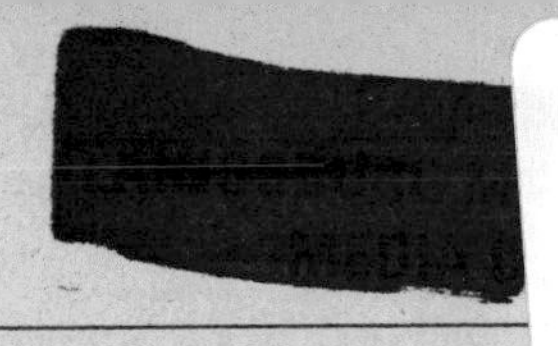

The Explosion

The chains that had been holding back his anger blew apart in an explosion the likes of which Derek had never imagined. Everything went white, and he could almost feel the windows rattle with his anger. In a moment he could hear the glass shattering around him, as a chair flew out of his hands and through the tall window. Then another chair—he spun it around and around and hurled it at the second window, bringing it down in ruins. Then a third chair rocketed through the final window. It crashed down with a deafening roar.

When it was done, and Derek turned back to the entrance, he saw his mother standing there wide-eyed, surrounded by her dinner guests and servants, but nobody dared approach him.

Then, just like that single explosive fist Derek had hurled at Mitch, Derek hurled something at his mother. It was far worse than a fist; it was the truth—a truth he had held locked away for two months. Now it came screaming out of the silence of the shattered room.

"YOU DIDN'T EVEN COME TO HIS FUNERAL!"

Derek stared her straight in the eye. "HE WAS THERE ALL ALONE—*I* WAS ALL ALONE—AND YOU DIDN'T EVEN COME!"

Books by Neal Shusterman

Dissidents
The Eyes of Kid Midas
Kid Heroes
Neon Angel—The Cherie Currie Story (with Cherie Currie)
The Shadow Club
Speeding Bullet
What Daddy Did

DISSIDENTS

NEAL SHUSTERMAN

A TOM DOHERTY ASSOCIATES BOOK
NEW YORK

DISSIDENTS

Cover art by Matthew Archambault

A Tor Book
Published by Tom Doherty Associates, Inc.
175 Fifth Avenue
New York, N.Y. 10010

ISBN: 0-812-53461-1
Library of Congress Catalog Card Number: 88–32525

First Tor edition: August 1994

Printed in the United States of America

0 9 8 7 6 5 4 3 2 1

For Lloyd, Jack, and Irvin,
the three wisemen, without
whose help and guidance I
would be up the creek-ski
without a paddle-ski, and for
Brad, who taught me the art
of slaying Dragons

Acknowledgments

This book would not have been possible without the invaluable help of Mr. and Mrs. Robert F. Ober, Jr., and Bradley Jarrett Fleishman. Their time spent with me attending to every little detail was more than I could have hoped for.

Thanks to Stephanie Owens Lurie for setting me on the right track (and keeping me from falling off the train).

And a special thanks to all the kids, both Soviet and American, whose comments and opinions helped to shape this book, chapter by chapter.

DISSIDENTS

dis·si·dent (dis ə dənt) *noun*
a dissenting person; one who disagrees with established rules and doctrines; a non-conformist.

CHAPTER I

What's Wrong with This Picture?

Derek was not about to let a simple change of address disturb his daily routine.

It was three o'clock, and at three o'clock it was time to play basketball. And so, equipped with his Sony Discman CD player, his Chicago Bulls jacket, and his Spalding leather basketball, Derek ventured out into the streets of Moscow.

Early in April, 1989; a bright and chilly day. In high spirits and with more energy than he was expected to have, Derek strode through the crowded streets, ignoring an incredible headache that never seemed to go away. He wandered between the rows of gray buildings in search of a court to play on, and maybe even someone to beat in a nice game of one-on-one. In the week that he had been in the Soviet Union, he had yet to come across a basket.

Today, Derek made his way toward the center of the city and found himself in yet another small park that seemed designed solely as a haven for the dark bronze statue in the middle of it. Although most of Moscow's parks were crowded and pleasant, this one was not. There were cold, uninviting benches by the paths, and only one was occupied—an old woman with big red cheeks and a heavy coat sat there, looking only a bit more content than the statue.

Derek bounced his ball across the cobblestone path of the park, dribbling carefully, because cobblestones made basketballs very unpredictable. He dribbled in circles, hopping to and fro, and managed to elude all the imaginary opponents before him.

"Ferretti takes the ball downcourt," he said for his own amusement. "Fifteen seconds left in the game, the Bulls down by one. Can Ferretti pull it off?"

The old woman looked at him as if he were crazy. He dribbled and turned, losing possession of the ball when it hit a crooked stone. He raced after it, catching it before it bounced off the path. "Ferretti regains possession of the ball with ten seconds left!" The old woman continued to stare at this spectacle, drawn in, no doubt, by the excitement of Derek's play-by-play sportscast. Derek faked to the right and drove toward the statue.

Before him, in the center of the small park, the dark bronze statue loomed like a frightening guardian of a mysterious culture—a man with a domed, bald head and a neat, pointed beard. Without looking at the face, Derek would have known who it was. All he had to see were the long coat and the dignified position of the hands, placed just so. It was Vladimir Ilyich Lenin, the most revered Comrade of them all.

Lenin, Derek had noticed, bore an odd resemblance to Oz, "the Great and Powerful." This was an observation he kept to himself, however, since such a comparison could get him into a great amount of trouble. Not only with the Soviet Union, but with his mother, who was infinitely more dangerous than the Kremlin.

"Five seconds remaining in the game! Can Ferretti do it?"

The look of power and determination in Mr. Lenin's face made him a wonderful opponent for Derek. Staring the statue in the eye, he dribbled low, using peripheral vision. He faked to the right, faked to the left. The statue was not deceived. Derek held the ball, then passed it to the statue. It bounced off the statue's chest, back to Derek, and Derek drove around Mr. Lenin to score. So much for stonewall defense.

"The crowd goes wild!" yelled Derek. "He's done it! With one second remaining, Derek 'Fireball' Ferretti sinks the final basket and says 'lights out' to Lenin's Red Brigade!" Derek cranked up the volume of the Discman CD player, which was already blasting into his brain, and began to sing along to the hard-rock tune.

The old woman with the red cheeks let her jaw drop open. She seemed about ready to have a coronary. Derek saw her mumble something to herself in annoyance.

Derek glanced back at Lenin the Great and Powerful, solemn guardian of all things Soviet. Lenin glared back down at Derek as if to say, "We are not amused by American teenagers dribbling basketballs and singing loudly in public."

It was as Derek was leaving the small park that he caught sight of it: a big black sedan way down the road, moving along with him, following his every move so obviously that it was almost a joke. It crept along like a slow black bull.

Derek was being followed—but today he was determined to shake them off his tail.

Derek faked to the right, and ducked down a thin

cold alley. The alley did not see much light and was still filled with patches of old hard snow. It had a damp smell to it, like all alleys. It could have been an alley anywhere in the world. It smelled like New York City, or Chicago—the two places where Derek had spent most of his fifteen years. Oddly enough, he was less frightened of the alleys here than of those back in the States.

Derek emerged from the alley and onto Olimpiyski Prospekt, "Olympic Avenue," a busy street that he recognized. From here he could find his way to wherever he wanted to go, and he knew where he was headed next. The black car spotted him once more as it came around the corner, and Derek hurried down the street to get away from it. Onward to Red Square.

The Kremlin was always great fun. Mainly because of the various reactions of the guards and militiamen as he got closer to Red Square. Some would completely ignore him, while others would make a fuss about his running by, watching him carefully as he passed. They would whisper among themselves in Russian, wondering if this dribbling American was some sort of threat to national security.

To Derek, being ignored was worse than being eyed suspiciously, and the Soviet Union was pretty good at treating Derek both ways. Half the time he was a dangerous spy, and the other half he simply didn't exist.

Derek finally reached the immense triangular fortress of the Kremlin, a walled city-within-a-city. Enclosed within that wall were the ancient buildings and gold-domed churches of the tsars, and the newer Palace of Congresses built by the Communist Party. (If it's a party, Derek once asked, then how come no one's dancing? His translator had decided not to translate that particular joke into Russian.) It was amazing to think that somewhere on the other side of the red-brick towers and walls of the Kremlin, most of the decisions of the Soviet Union were made, so close to Derek and his basketball.

To his right, at the visitors' entrance to the Kremlin, stood two white-gloved guards. For three days, Derek had come up to these two men, dribbling his ball, trying to get a reaction from them. He would dribble in a circle, and between his legs; then he would look at the guards. Nothing. He would dribble high, dribble low, throw the ball into the air, catch it on his index finger, and spin it. No reaction. The guards completely ignored him.

Then, yesterday, Derek dribbled up to the guards, and one of them just stuck out his hand and grabbed the ball away. The guard, who was a full head taller than Derek's five-foot-two, held the ball tightly, looked at Derek with dark brown Soviet eyes, and said two English words, with the heaviest of Russian accents.

"Double dribble," he said. Then he smiled and handed the ball back to Derek. The other guard laughed, and Derek had smiled as well. In the week he had been in the Soviet Union, no Soviet had smiled at him. Not that they didn't smile—they did, but never at him.

That was yesterday. Now Derek had enough respect for those guards not to bother them anymore. Instead, Derek turned left, and dribbled down the half-mile-long Kremlin wall, pressing on toward Red Square. The black car, which had found him again, followed him all the way, staying twenty yards behind.

When Derek reached the end of the Kremlin wall, he could see the huge cobblestone expanse of Red Square, bounded on the far end by Saint Basil's Cathedral.

Derek liked Saint Basil's; it was like no other cathedral he had ever seen. It had tall spires and domes that swirled with bright colors—red, blue, yellow, and green—and each spire was covered with textures that caught deep intricate shadows. Every dome bulged, then tapered, like an onion, and swirled toward a gold crown, topped with a gold cross. The swirling colors of the domes gave the illusion that they were spinning ever so slightly. At first sight, a few days before, Derek had noted that Saint Basil's sort of looked like a weird collection of giant Dairy Queen cones. He didn't tell anyone this, because he didn't want to sound *too* stupid.

Derek slowed and stopped at the edge of Red Square, holding his basketball, thinking what his next move should be. There were groups of militiamen hanging around as if they had nothing to do. None of them took notice of Derek, but he could swear plain-clothed KGB men were watching him. (The KGB, Derek knew, was like the CIA, only worse—which was hard to imagine. In most movies, the CIA were the bad guys, unless there were Russians in the movie. Then the CIA were the good guys, and the KGB were the bad guys.)

Derek never had the guts to dribble his basketball in Red Square, mostly because of Lenin's tomb. The red marble monument, which rested by the back wall of the Kremlin, always had a long, snaking line of people waiting to pay their respects to their leader, whose body lay beyond the big black doors of the monument, preserved eternally in a glass casket for all to see. No one would dare to speak near the tomb, much less dribble a basketball toward it; the tomb guards probably had orders to shoot to kill, or something like that.

Still, the idea of dribbling right through Red Square was very tempting. It would certainly be an obnoxious thing to do, but that had never stopped Derek before. He was fifteen—he could still get away with being obnoxious.

It was a scary prospect, thinking of the sort of trouble it could get him into. He had heard the story of some Westerner who had, just for fun, flown a plane over Soviet airspace and landed in Red Square. "He was up the creek-ski without a paddle-ski," Derek's father had said. On the other hand, what was so bad about dribbling a basketball in a public square? But on the other hand, Ralphy Sherman, an old friend from home, had once told Derek that the Russians punish kids by spooning out their eyeballs and serving them for dinner in borscht. (Of course, Ralphy Sherman also claimed that he had swum in molten lava during his trip to Hawaii, so no one much trusted what Ralphy Sherman said, but you never know. . . .)

Derek turned to see that the black car was nowhere in sight, because no vehicles were allowed in Red Square. If Derek were going to dribble across the square, it was now or never. He took a deep breath, cranked up the music in his ears, and raced off toward the far corner of Red Square.

Dribbling as fast as he could, and keeping as far away from Lenin's tomb as possible, Derek wove in and out of the crowds until they thinned.

A minute later, Derek found himself in the center of the square, alone, just one single American boy bouncing a ball for all of Moscow to see. The cool April wind brushed across his face as he pressed on, moving closer and closer to the far end of the famous square.

As he neared the far corner, an odd sense of accomplishment overcame him. He had actually done it! He must have been the first American ever to dribble a basketball across Red Square. Surely that deserved a place in the *Guinness Book of World Records*. He wove through the crowds at the end of the square, and raced past St. Basil's (which, Derek noted, not only resembled a bumper crop of Dairy Queen cones, but also looked a bit like "It's a Small World" in Disneyland).

Just when Derek thought he'd got off scot-free, something unexpected happened . . . something that had to do with his brand-new high-top all-star white leather basketball shoes. Derek was in the habit of wearing his high-tops loose and untied one hundred percent of the time. Of course he always tucked in the laces, but laces never liked to stay tucked in. More often than not, they trailed along the ground behind him. It never bothered him much, except for those rare occasions when he tripped on them. Like now.

Derek went flying head over heels, and the basketball flew out of his hands. The black car screeched to a halt in front of him, and the basketball rebounded off the car door and back to Derek. He grabbed the ball, and stood to face the music.

They had found him, and there was nowhere he could run.

Now he was in for it. Up the creek-ski, without a paddle-ski.

A window squeaked down, and inside the big black car two men wearing reflecting sunglasses peered out at Derek. Neither one seemed too happy.

"Derek," said the man closest to him, "you're a royal pain, you know that?"

"Just keeping busy," said Derek, still bouncing his ball.

"You're driving everyone crazy! Why don't you slow down for once? Just relax!"

"Can't relax! Gotta keep busy!" Derek smoothly dribbled the ball between his legs. Keeping busy was very important. Derek had his reasons, and he didn't have to explain them to anyone. He smiled at the two men in the car. "Wanna play basketball?" he asked, more to be obnoxious than anything else.

The man closest to him took off his glasses and peered at Derek with an American sort of sternness quite different from that of the guards, the old woman, or the statue of Lenin. His name was Jim Briggs, but Derek called him Big Jim. He was from somewhere in the Midwest, had huge shoulders and bad breath. The one driving the car was Harold Welch, the family chauffeur. Harold didn't talk very much. He just carried a gun.

"Your mother won't be happy," said Big Jim.

"Listen, have you ever thought that if you weren't following me all the time, I might not be such a royal pain?"

"It's my job to follow you, Derek," said Big Jim.

Derek began dribbling once more. "I don't need a bodyguard," he said, which was absolutely true, as far as Derek was concerned. So, he was the ambassador's son. Big deal. No other American in Moscow had, or needed, a bodyguard. His mom said it was for his protection, but Derek knew the truth: it was to keep Derek out of trouble. She didn't trust him, plain and simple.

"You don't know the language, or your way around, Derek," said Big Jim, as if he were talking to a small child. That always made Derek angry.

"What are they going to do? Lock me in the Kremlin dungeon, and spoon out my eyeballs? They don't do that stuff," he said. ". . . anymore," he added.

"Don't be so sure," said Harold-the-Gun.

Derek's eyeballs began to hurt at just the thought of it.

"You should consider yourself lucky," said Big Jim. "How many kids even get to have a bodyguard?"

"Yeah," said Derek, "I'm real lucky." He turned to look at the people around Red Square. Far across was a group of kids on their way home from school. A bit closer were a boy and girl a year or two older than Derek, talking and laughing together. These were people he could not talk to, because he didn't know their language. Even if he could talk to them, what would he say? What would they have to say to him? As long as Derek had to answer to Big Jim and Harold-the-Gun, Derek was afraid he would never find out. If it were up to his mother, he would spend all his life either at home, or at the Anglo-American School. No contact with the outside world. Ever. And it wasn't easy to keep busy when you couldn't even go out into the street.

"All right," said Derek. "Maybe you guys can be useful after all." He spun the ball on his finger. "Tell me where I can find a basketball court."

"The Anglo-American School gym . . ."

"I don't want to use the Anglo-American School gym," said Derek. "The floor is sticky, and it smells like puke. Why can't I play basketball where the Soviet kids play?"

Big Jim didn't answer him; he just shook his head in the same way the old woman had. Perhaps Americans and Soviets weren't that different, after all. They all seemed to have the same opinion of Derek.

Derek knew for a fact that the Soviets played basketball but, try as he might, he couldn't seem to find a single park that had a basketball court. The Anglo-American School gym, aside from being sticky and smelling awful, was filled with older American and British kids this time of the day—kids whom he already disliked. When school started on Monday, after Easter vacation, he'd have more than enough time with them. Now Derek wanted some time to play ball with Soviet kids, and he was getting pretty annoyed that no one would let him.

Still no answer from Big Jim. "It's almost dinner-time, Derek," Big Jim finally said. "Why don't you come with us?"

Derek sighed, tossed the ball in the back seat, and got in. Just like his father had always said, it's impossible to get an answer from someone who works for a government.

CHAPTER 2

My Mother, the Ambassador

Spaso House was perhaps the most beautiful and largest private residence in all of Moscow, and living there was the best part of being the American ambassador's son. With its big front lawn and American flag hanging above the entranceway, Spaso House looked like a miniature version of the White House—only it was yellow—canary yellow, with white columns around the semicircular porch. Spaso House was, in fact, so yellow that to Derek it also looked like something from Disneyland, but he liked it all the same. It was a mansion, and whatever color it was, Derek was more than happy to live in a mansion. Besides, a Disneyland-yellow mansion was a pleasant relief from the dull gray apartment buildings that filled the rest of Moscow. He just wished it wasn't called Spaso House.

"*Spa-ssuh* House," his younger sister Dayna always corrected, "not *Spaz-o* House," but Derek still couldn't get the pronunciation right.

Spaso House was quite a change from the modest two-bedroom apartment Derek had shared with his father back in Chicago. He liked his old apartment, though, and would have been very happy to stay there with his father for a long, long time.

But no one expected his father to die.

No one ever expects a car accident.

Since then, Derek kept himself very, very busy, thinking about anything and everything else but his father. Basketball in the gray streets of Moscow was a fine way to keep busy.

This, however, was to be Derek's last day of street basketball. When Harold-the-Gun and Big Jim dropped Derek off that afternoon, Derek's mother and sister were just starting dinner, tired of waiting for him. Big Jim called his mother out of the room to brief her on Derek's "delinquent" activities, while Derek sat across from his sister in the formal dining room. The exotic antique table seated ten, but today there were only the three of them.

"You're in a mess of trouble," said Dayna as their mother left the room with Big Jim. "Mom's really mad at you this time!"

Derek shrugged. "So what else is new?" It seemed she had been mad at him since the moment he arrived. At the airport she had greeted him with a weak half-human hug that was too short and didn't seem warm enough for a mother who hadn't seen her son in a year. She had never been one to show great affection, and now, surrounded by dignitaries and officials—even at the moment of Derek's arrival—she seemed all the more uncomfortable hugging him. She made no mention of Derek's dad—not a single word. Most people say things like "I'm so sorry about your father," but his mom said nothing. You'd think she might—after all, they'd only been divorced for four years—but no, not Ambassador Beatrice Wilder-Ferretti. Not a word. She dealt with unpleasant topics by ignoring them.

She wasn't even Beatrice Wilder-Ferretti anymore; she had dropped the Ferretti from her name right after the divorce. Even his sister had changed her last name to Wilder when they both came over to the Soviet Union last year. Derek guessed that, with his father gone, he was the last Ferretti left—and he wasn't about to change his name to Wilder, too.

As Derek sat at the long table in the fancy oval room, he could hear his mother and Big Jim talking next door. Derek had been dumped in Big Jim's hands from the moment he arrived in Moscow, and they had hated each other from the onset.

"Keep him entertained," his mom had told Jim. Everyone knew how important it was to keep Derek entertained, with his father gone only three weeks.

Jim had tried to pass himself off as something like a camp counselor, which was like hiring Darth Vader as a babysitter. Besides, counselors didn't wear three-piece suits and travel around in cars with bulletproof glass.

On those first two days, Jim had showed Derek around, giving him a tourist's view of Moscow—like a class trip, all the museums and things. It was fascinating, and might have even been fun, if Derek had been with someone he liked.

On both of those days, after the museums, Jim had hurried Derek back to Spaso House, where Derek waited for his mother to be done with all of her diplomatic duties—which was never.

On the third day, Derek decided he would rather play basketball.

Ambassador Wilder's conversation with Big Jim the Bodyguard ended, and she marched calmly back into the dining room. Derek was prepared for the worst. He watched as she sat down gracefully, replaced the napkin on her lap, and then turned to Derek.

"There's no excuse for the way you're acting," she said. "Absolutely no excuse." She stared at him with those cold eagle eyes. They were definitely the eyes of an ambassador, no doubt about it.

Dayna was not above putting her two cents in, either. "Everyone says you're an embarrassment," she said, as she ate some sort of pickled fish that could not possibly taste as awful as it smelled. "That's what everyone says."

"Oh yeah?" said Derek. His twelve-year-old sister was not about to call him an embarrassment. "Who's everyone?"

"Everyone important," she answered.

"It's not a good impression to start off with," said his mother. "As the ambassador's son, there are certain ways you're supposed to act, and certain ways you are not. You *did* want to come here and live with us, didn't you?"

Derek nodded. It was true; he did. After the funeral, they had given Derek a choice: live with his mother the big-time-hotshot-first-female-American-ambassador-to-the-Soviet-Union, or go live with Aunt May and Uncle Richard, who didn't want him at all. The choice was easy.

"Jim said that you threw your basketball at a statue of Lenin."

Derek shrugged, "I didn't throw my basketball *at* it; I passed the ball *to* it. It was a game."

"You had better learn to be a little more respectful, and a little less defiant," said his mother, as Svetlana, their cook, brought everyone a bowl of borscht. Borscht, Derek knew, was beet soup, a red-purple liquid. It didn't have eyeballs in it, as Ralphy Sherman said it would, but Derek still thought it was the most disgusting invention since lima beans. His mother had said that it took some getting used to, but now they ate it all the time. His mom and Dayna spooned it up like it was Campbell's soup. Derek couldn't watch.

"Things are tense in Moscow these days," his mom continued. "It's best to keep a low profile until everyone grows used to you. Perhaps when you settle in, you can have a little more leeway, but until then, no more basketball in the streets. Is that understood?"

Derek didn't answer right away.

"Is that understood, Derek?"

"It's a free country . . . ," said Derek, using one of his favorite expressions. Unfortunately, now that they were in the Soviet Union, the expression didn't sit very well with his mother. She stared at him with that "think again" sort of look on her face. His sister laughed.

"Anyway it's not like Gorbachoff is gonna stick his head out of the Kremlin and yell at me."

"*Gorbachev*, not *Gorbachoff*," corrected Dayna, shaking her head. "Mikhail Sergeyevich Gorbachev," and then she added, "but his good friends call him 'Gorby.' "

"Yeah," said Derek, snidely, "but his *real* good friends call him 'Mikey.' "

"I don't know what to do with you, Derek," said his mother, shaking her head and daintily munching her smelly fish. Derek looked at his plate. For the first time in his life, he finished his vegetables first.

"Maybe it's culture shock," she said, sighing.

"Maybe it's cabin fever," said Derek.

"What?"

"You know," he said, "cabin fever from being locked

in a little room for a whole week. It's like I'm in prison!"

"Stop exaggerating!"

"Well, it is! Wherever I go, Big Jim follows me, like I'm a criminal or something." As far as Derek was concerned, Big Jim was one of the worst things about his new life. He had told his mother how he felt, but she didn't seem to care. He had even told Philip Winn, his mother's aide. Philip said he would do something about Big Jim, but nothing had happened.

"I don't want him following me all the time!" Derek realized that his voice was getting a bit too loud. Svetlana's eyes darted back and forth nervously as she filled everyone's water glasses.

"Can't you just calm down?" said his mother, patiently.

"Yeah, just mellow out," said Dayna.

"Remember, you're an American in the Soviet Union. You have to set an example."

"An example for whom? Big Jim doesn't even let me meet any Soviets! Why can't I meet any Soviet kids?" asked Derek.

"There are more than enough kids at the Anglo-American School . . . ," said his mom.

"But what about Soviet kids? Big Jim won't let me talk to anybody without him standing behind me," said Derek. "Boy, what a way to meet somebody. Hi, I'm Derek. Here's my personal security guard. You wanna be my friend?"

"You can't be left alone!"

"Why not?"

"You need protection!"

"From whom?"

"From any number of Soviets who are anti-American!"

"Give it up, Mom!" he said, not believing any of her diplomatic answers. "We all know the only reason Big Jim follows me is because you don't trust me alone!" Derek stared at his mom, and she stared him down, like a good ambassador should. Then she turned to her plate, finishing off her fish. Derek tasted his. It didn't taste as bad as it smelled.

"Maybe you'd rather go back to Aunt May and Uncle Richard," his mother suggested quietly.

Derek gritted his teeth at the thought. He had stayed with his aunt and uncle for only two weeks, and he swore he could still smell the mothballs that were everywhere in the house. Perhaps the mothballs had gotten into his blood. Maybe that's why he still had a headache. Their small house didn't have room for a fifteen-year-old. Derek always felt as though he was in the way, like an unwanted pet. Although he would never admit it, Derek often wondered whether or not he was just a bad kid. Maybe that's why his aunt and uncle didn't want him. Because he was a bad kid. Maybe that was the reason for a whole lot of things.

"You don't want me here, do you?" he asked his mother. He couldn't look up at her—he just gazed down at his half-eaten fish and untouched bowl of borscht, feeling his miserable headache grow.

"Of course I want you here, Derek." Just hearing her say it made him feel a whole lot better. "But you don't seem to be happy here."

Derek didn't answer her. In many ways he *was* happy. Now that his father was gone, he wanted to be with his mom more than anything else in the world—but at the same time, there was Big Jim and everything else making life miserable. School started up on Monday; it wasn't going to be like school back in Chicago, but whatever it was like, he would have to finish up tenth grade, and perhaps all of high school, there. It was frightening. Much more frightening to Derek than the streets of Moscow. But life here was better than being an unwanted pet in Chicago.

"I'm sorry," said Derek, still not looking up from his plate. "I'll try to do better."

"No more basketball in the streets?"

Derek nodded. "No more basketball in the streets."

"No more annoying Kremlin guards?"

"Agreed," said Derek.

"Good. When school starts, Harold will drive you home, and I expect you to stay on the grounds," she said. "No more traipsing around the streets of Moscow at all."

"But, Mom . . ."

"But nothing! After what you did today, you should be glad you're not in more trouble. If the Soviet officials had caught you, you'd be in hot water!"

"If *they* caught you, you'd end up like Yuri," added Dayna.

"Who?"

Dayna dropped her jaw open, and looked at Derek with her favorite "boy-are-you-stupid" expression. "You mean you don't know about Yuri, the world-famous Soviet dissident? Where have you been?"

"Chicago," said Derek.

"That explains it," answered his sister. "Yuri Shafiroff," she began, as if reciting from some encyclopedia in her overactive little brain, "was exiled to Siberia ten years ago, and then was expelled to Romania, where the government is so nasty, it makes Moscow look like Mr. Roger's Neighborhood."

"Oh!" said Derek. "You mean *Shafiroff*! Why didn't you just say so? Everybody knows about Shafiroff." It was true. One of the networks had even done a TV movie about him.

"Well," said Dayna, "we hear about him so much, we just call him by his first name." Then she added, "You would have known who I was talking about if you read newspapers!"

Derek didn't try to get back at her for that last crack, because she was right. For the son of an ambassador, Derek was pretty behind on current events—unless they involved sports scores.

"And that's what will happen to you if you don't listen to Mom!" threatened Dayna.

"You're lying, Dayna," said Derek. "They can't do anything bad to me; I've got *diplomatic immunity*, don't I?"

"Yes, you do," said his mother. "But you could make things difficult for the embassy, and I won't let you do that. So once school starts, you stay out of the streets."

Derek looked down. So now he was responsible for his entire country's image. What an annoying responsibility. He silently gave in to his mother's demand by nodding.

"Good, that's settled," said Ambassador Wilder. "Now be a good boy, and eat your borscht."

As usual, Ambassador Wilder left right after dinner, to go to some sort of diplomatic party, which seemed to be all she ever did. If it wasn't a party here at Spaso House, it was a party somewhere else. What a life. Party till you drop. Who ever thought an ambassador's life would be like that?

In the week that Derek had been in Moscow, there had been two small parties at Spaso House, and six more were on the agenda for the month. Derek didn't mind the parties. So far, anyway. With the exception of caviar and borscht, the food was always good.

Now, as twilight began to dim, Derek wandered through the huge two-story mansion, trying to forget about the scolding he had just received. He marveled at the architecture and grimaced at the sight of the two ugly wooden statues near the entrance of the Ballroom. One was of an Indian, the other was someone's questionable interpretation of Columbia, goddess of Liberty. They were perhaps the tackiest things he had ever seen.

In the Chandelier Room, with its high vaulted ceiling and tall white columns, his sister practiced piano. Like everything else Dayna did, she did it flawlessly, and it annoyed Derek no end. Little Miss Perfect. Her music rose up past the immense chandelier, to the elaborate designs carved into the curved ceiling. The piece was classical—the only kind of music that could be played in a room like that.

Derek much preferred the Knoll Room, on the other side of the house. It was warmer, and had a homier feeling, like his apartment in Chicago. The furniture was modern, set on huge Persian rugs. There were tall windows that made it one of the brightest rooms in the house, and a large fireplace to keep it warm through the endless Soviet winters. Against one wall was the huge wooden tiller of a boat, and against another wall was a television with a VCR and a pile of videotapes brought in from the U.S.A. He had already put in a request for all the James Bond movies he could get. Even though he had seen them all countless times already, Derek suspected that those videos were going to be very important to him while he was confined in the silent halls of Spaso House.

It wasn't like being back in the States, where he could call any number of friends and go over to their house, or walk to the park and play basketball, or just hang out at the video arcade. Those days were done and gone. The problem was that the new days hadn't begun yet, either.

Derek walked slowly across the floor of the Knoll Room. His sister's playing was distant, and he could hear the wood beneath his feet creaking. Should he watch TV, he thought, or should he explore his immense house? Should he put on his Discman and blast his brain out? In his present mood, Derek didn't feel like doing much of anything at all, so he lay down on the couch and let his mind wander.

There were very few American kids in Moscow. The Anglo-American school had about one hundred and fifty kids, but only about thirty of them were high-school age. Derek had already had the "pleasure" of meeting seven of the thirty kids with whom he'd be spending the rest of the year. He had met them by accident two days ago, during his daily trip through the streets in search of a basket.

It was somewhere around Kalinin Prospekt, one of the busiest streets of Moscow, that Derek had stumbled upon a group of kids actually speaking English.

"Hey," said Derek, stopping right in front of them. "Are you guys Americans?" There were four boys and three girls. The biggest one, wearing a Notre Dame jacket, stepped up to Derek. He was at least seventeen, and stood almost six feet tall. He looked Derek up and down, as if there were something wrong with Derek. In fact, all the kids looked at Derek that way.

They stared at him coldly for a few more seconds, and then the big one in the Notre Dame jacket, without as much as a smile, said, "Nice CD player. It would get a good price on the black market."

Derek didn't know what to say to that, so he ignored

it. "Hi, I'm Derek," he said as pleasantly as he could. "Do you live here in Moscow, or are you tourists, or what?"

The unpleasant leader of this unpleasant little group gently took the earphones off Derek's head. "Mind?" he asked.

Derek shrugged, and Notre Dame took the Discman away from him, to listen to it. He then passed it to the other kids in the group. Notre Dame nodded. "Cool tunes," he said approvingly.

"Where the hell is Fyodor?" mumbled one of the others.

"Shut up," said Notre Dame. He grabbed Derek's ball. "Spalding!" he said. "And a new one, too." He began dribbling, and Derek began to get nervous, particularly because his Discman had disappeared.

"I should get going," said Derek. Notre Dame looked at him, but didn't say anything right away. The rest ignored Derek, either giggling to themselves or looking around for this Theodore person.

"You know," said Notre Dame, "I lost a ball just like this the other day. Maybe this is it."

Derek knew he was lying, and also knew he would have to fight to get his Discman and basketball back—but seven against one was not very good odds. Thinking quickly, Derek looked over Notre Dame's shoulder, smiled and waved. "Hey, Theodore," he said. "How ya doing?"

No one was tricked.

"Nice try," said Notre Dame. "But that's Fyodor, with an *F*." The two stared at each other, and Derek clenched his fists, ready for a fight.

"Any problem here?" said Big Jim, who had come up behind Derek.

"No, not at all," Notre Dame said coolly, as he handed

Derek his ball. "Don't tell me," he said; "you're the ambassador's son, right?"

Derek nodded.

"It figures," said Notre Dame. "We heard you were coming." Someone in the group behind him quickly gave back his Discman. "Thanks for letting us listen to your CD player," said Notre Dame. Now it was Derek's turn not to say anything. He just stared this bully of a kid down.

"See you around," said Notre Dame, but his eyes said, *Wait till I catch you without your bodyguard.*

"Yeah, see you around," said Derek, returning the same nasty look. Derek left with Big Jim, leaving Notre Dame to light up a cigarette.

As they walked away, Jim had turned to Derek and said, "That's Mitch! He'll be one of your friends at the Anglo-American school."

That had been Derek's one and only run-in with his schoolmates. Pretty pathetic specimens, Derek thought. He hoped the Soviets didn't think all American kids were like that.

From what Derek was able to find out from his sister, the American kids at the school stuck pretty close together, and Mitch's group seemed like the clique to be in. This *Fyodor*, Derek also found out, was probably the only Soviet teen the American kids knew. Fyodor was a black-marketeer; Mitch and his friends would get American things from the embassy commissary, such as food and cigarettes, and sell them to Fyodor, who would, in turn, sell them to other Soviets. Everyone knew that selling American products in Russia was, for the most part, illegal, and that is why it was called the black market.

"How's your headache today?" asked a voice behind

him, as Derek lay there on the couch, deep in his own thoughts.

Derek opened his eyes. Around him, the Knoll Room had gotten very dark and was beginning to get cold. Philip Winn stood by the fireplace, trying to light a fire. Derek was glad it was Philip rather than one of the many servants that wove in and out of the house. Philip was the ambassador's chief aide, and as the ambassador's right-hand man, Philip had his own little apartment right there in Spaso House, so he could often be found in the rooms of the main house.

"My headache?" said Derek. "It's the same."

"Need any aspirin?"

"No, thanks." Derek had gotten used to his headache—he had almost forgotten it was there. At first the doctors thought it was a remnant of his concussion from the car accident, but it never went away. Derek had learned to live with it day after day, without telling many people about it. Philip was the only person in Moscow who knew about Derek's headache. He was the only one whom Derek really liked.

"Did you hear?" said Derek, as he sprawled out on the large couch. "I'm grounded for life."

"I heard," said Philip. "Don't worry; your mom's just concerned about you. In a few weeks things will lighten up—you'll see. You and your mom will have a regular détente, I'll bet."

Derek grabbed the remote control and clicked on the TV. A Soviet newscaster babbled about something that Derek, more than likely, couldn't care less about, even if he *could* speak Russian.

"Did my sister ever get grounded like that?" asked Derek. Dayna, who landed with their mother after the divorce, had been in Moscow since his mother's appointment last year.

"Well," said Philip, "you and your sister are two different people."

"In other words," translated Derek, "she's a good little girl, and I'm a bad little boy."

"No," said Philip, "you're just different, that's all."

Derek sighed. He wished he could believe that.

"Dayna had problems when she got here, too," offered Philip.

"Oh yeah? Like what?"

"Well . . . ," said Philip, searching for something to say, "Well . . . she got sick from drinking the water!"

Derek had to laugh. No, his sister was a perfect little girl and never got into trouble. Derek was the only one who ever did anything wrong, and everyone knew it. Even his father. Derek's headache began to get worse as he thought about it, so he turned up the volume on the TV. A woman in a hospital bed, with bags under her eyes, was talking to a reporter; then the interview went to a Soviet girl who seemed to be Derek's age.

That caught Derek's attention.

He sat up and watched closely, unable to understand a word she said. If his sister was there, she would've bragged about how she understood most of it, and how she was almost fluent in Russian.

The girl and the reporter both jabbered away. To Derek it probably would have sounded the same if it were played in reverse.

"What's this about?" asked Derek. "Who's she?"

"That's Anna Shafiroff," said Philip, who also spoke fluent Russian. "Yuri Shafiroff's daughter."

"Shafiroff the dissident?"

"None other," said Philip. "Kind of pretty, isn't she?"

Kind of pretty? She was gorgeous! Long black hair and big brown eyes. Derek had always thought that Soviet girls would look like fat men with wigs and with hair all over their legs. He sure was wrong. True, there were some ugly people in the Soviet Union, but there were just as many ugly people in Chicago.

"What's she saying?" asked Derek.

"She's talking about her father. The Soviet government has offered him the chance to return to Moscow, but he won't come. Anna's mother is dying, and Anna can't understand why her father won't return. They haven't seen him in over five years."

Anna spoke with strength, but there was sadness in her voice as well. Her voice sounded almost musical.

"How awful!" said Derek. What a terrible thing, not seeing your father for five years!

Then Anna was gone from the screen as quickly as she had appeared, and the dull newscaster jabbered on about something else. Derek lowered the volume.

"A sad story," said Philip, and then he added, "It sort of puts things into perspective, and makes you realize how lucky you are."

Derek thought about that. "At least her father's alive," he said quietly. Philip had no answer for that one.

Derek closed his eyes and idly thought of Anna Shafiroff. He wondered how much it hurt *her* when she thought of her father. He wondered if she got headaches, too.

CHAPTER 3

Derek Fails the Test

On the first day of school Derek had several tests, none of which took place in the classroom. The tests weren't even given by teachers. These particular tests were administered by a senior in a Notre Dame jacket.

During first period, Derek met all the high-school kids, which didn't take very long. Mitch, who never seemed to take off his Notre Dame jacket, shook Derek's hand, but it wasn't a normal handshake. Mitch kept squeezing harder and harder, as if it were a contest to see who was stronger.

"Don't mind Mitch," said one of the other kids; "he's just like that. He'll test you until he gets to know you."

But Derek found out there was more to Mitch than just being "like that," and the little tests Mitch gave new kids were very important. Mitch was the undisputed leader of the school. He and his gang of six patrolled the school like the KGB, and you had to be approved by Mitch if you wanted to have friends.

During his first day of classes, Derek had three more run-ins with Mitch—three more "tests." Derek flunked the first two.

Test one: between classes, Mitch went out of his way to bump his heavy shoulder against Derek in the hall.

"Aren't you going to say you're sorry?" Mitch asked.

"Why should I?" said Derek. "*You* bumped into *me*." Derek wasn't about to bow down to him and to apologize for something he didn't do.

"Oh," said Mitch. "You think you're better than me just because your mom's an ambassador?"

"No," said Derek, "I think I'm better than you because *you're* an asshole."

Another kid laughed, and Mitch smiled. It wasn't a pleasant smile—it was the kind of smile a crocodile had before snapping its victim in two.

"You're a pretty funny guy," said Mitch, still smiling. "Hope you like it here." Mitch turned and sauntered off like a guy who had everything under control. And he did.

Test two: At lunch not a single kid his age would sit with Derek. Mitch had put the word out that Derek was not approved, and no one dared go against what Mitch said.

Derek quietly sat and ate his lunch, surrounded by seven- and eight-year-olds, the only ones who would sit at the table with him.

And then, to rub it in, Mitch came by his table. "Hi, Derek," he said with the nastiest of smiles. "I didn't realize you were still in the third grade." From across the room Derek heard snickers from some of the other high-school kids. Derek wouldn't look at them.

"I came over here," said Mitch, slowly, "because I

thought you might want to apologize for calling me a name before."

Derek smiled and said, with a mouthful of food, "I call it the way I see it."

Mitch nodded, raised his eyebrows and said, "Enjoy your lunch." Then he slowly sauntered back to his table, leaving Derek to eat among eight-year-olds.

"You're an idiot," Dayna whispered as Derek left the cafeteria. "If you don't pass Mitch's test, you won't have any friends."

"Then I guess I won't have any friends," said Derek.

TEST NUMBER three: This one, Derek figured, was the final exam. It was right before the last period. Derek had gone to the bathroom, and Mitch came in, grabbing Derek and pushing him against the hard tiles of the wall, holding him there.

Derek had been beaten up in a school bathroom once before. In fifth grade, he had been beaten up by three sixth-graders because he'd spit out of a window, and it had landed on their heads. Derek figured that by high school everyone was more mature. Apparently not.

Well, thought Derek, *I won't go down without a fight* . . . , but fighting wasn't quite what Mitch had in mind.

"You had best get something straight," said Mitch, holding Derek against the wall. "There are certain rules we go by in this school. First of all, we always apologize when we bump someone in the hall."

"You mean when *you* bump someone," corrected Derek. Mitch slammed him against the wall again. Derek struggled to get free, but Mitch was simply too big.

"Second," said Mitch, "we do not curse out our classmates. It's bad manners."

Derek didn't say anything.

"You see," said Mitch, "this school is like a big family, and we don't like new kids with bad attitudes." Mitch waited for Derek to respond, but Derek wouldn't give him the satisfaction.

Mitch loosened his grip on Derek, but just a little.

"I'm telling you this because I like you," said Mitch.

Derek could have laughed at that. *Yeah,* thought Derek, *and I'm the Easter Bunny!*

". . . and since I like you," continued Mitch, "I'll give you a second chance to make it up to me." Mitch let Derek go, and stepped back, leaning against the door of the stall.

"All you have to do," said Mitch, "is say that you're sorry for bumping me in the hall, and that you're sorry for calling me a name. Do that, and you can be part of our family."

Mitch waited, and Derek clenched his teeth. Mitch had tried to steal his CD player, steal his ball, steal his newfound friends, and now he wanted Derek to apologize for it. Now Mitch was stealing something much more valuable: Derek's self-respect.

"Well," said Mitch, "what's it gonna be?"

Derek looked away. It was a hard pill to swallow—but if his life at the Anglo-American school was going to be bearable, he realized he'd have to go along with it, and apologize. *They're only words,* Derek told himself. *Just because I say them, doesn't mean I have to* feel *them.*

"All right," said Derek. "I'm sorry. I apologize, all right? Happy now?" There, he had done it. As much as it hurt, he had spit out the awful words, sacrificing his self-respect for admission into the Anglo-American crowd.

Mitch smiled at his nauseating little victory. "Good," he said. "That's a good boy. I'll see you back in class."

But there in class, Derek discovered that nothing had changed. Even with Mitch's "approval," they all still treated Derek like he had the plague. Like he was some sort of outcast. Like he didn't deserve to have any friends.

It was during that last period that Derek made his decision. If he wasn't good enough for them, then they weren't good enough for him. He didn't want them for his friends. Not a single one of them.

DEREK DISAPPEARED from sight when he got home. He didn't go to his room; he didn't go out; he simply disappeared. He sat, hidden by a gray shower curtain, in a bathtub that nobody used, in the cold, vacant guest wing of Spaso House.

He wasn't taking a bath—his clothes were on and the water wasn't. He was here because it was the farthest away he could possibly go. In the house, he could block out Moscow, but that wasn't enough. In the guest wing, he could block out his mother and sister, but that wasn't enough. In the bathtub, shrouded by the gray curtain, he could block out *everything* except his own mind and soul . . . and so he sat there alone, because being alone by himself seemed better than being alone while surrounded by people.

He was not being busy.

He was simply tired of being busy, and so here he sat, after his first miserable day at school, in the dim light of the bathroom.

His headache had reached new extremes today, and no matter how hard he tried to relax, it wouldn't go away. There was something else behind the headache, however. Something he couldn't let anyone see. It was a feeling of anger that lived in him, growing like a monster, spreading ugly tentacles through his arms and legs. Worming through his mind. Anger that had no reason and no direction. "The Dragon" is what his dad used to call it. Derek's temper. Sometimes it seemed as if Derek's Dragon had a life of its own.

At that moment Derek was angry at everything and everyone in the world, and he had to get his anger under control. He had to push it way down, because if he didn't he was afraid he might explode.

The anger ran so strong and so deep that Derek imagined that, if he concentrated hard enough, he could blow out all the windows of the house in a fiery explosion. He could almost hear the shattering of glass.

But something else broke the silence. A soft, desperate whisper.

Dad, they don't want me here. They don't want me, and they don't like me. What should I do?

Derek's father had once promised him he would always be there, and his father was not one to break a promise—not if he could help it. Derek didn't know about God, or the afterlife or any of that, but there was one thing he did know: if there were a way, his father would be there listening to him in the damp mildewed air of the old tub.

But what if he wasn't there? That was the other possibility, and it was too horrible for Derek to imagine. What if his father was never going to listen? Ever?

Or what if his father was there, but didn't want to help him? That was the worst thought of all.

"Tell me what to do, Dad. Please. Tell me," he whispered, and waited for an answer—not an answer he could hear, but one he could feel. But instead of an answer, Derek heard the sound of the curtain being ripped aside. Standing there right in front of him was Philip Winn.

"Derek! What are you doing here?" he asked. "We've been looking all over for you! We thought you'd run away!"

"Where would I run to?" mumbled Derek.

Philip gazed down at Derek, who looked utterly ridiculous sitting there in the dry bathtub. "I guess you didn't have a good day in school, huh?"

"Yeah, you could say that," Derek said, figuring that to be the understatement of the century. Philip sat on the edge of the bathtub, and Derek wouldn't look at him. If he did, his anger would fly out at Philip too, and Philip would know how much he was holding inside. Philip already knew about his headaches; that was enough.

"No one ever said this was going to be easy," said Philip.

"Save it," said Derek. "I've heard it all before."

". . . and I know how you felt about your father. . . ."

"Leave my father out of this!" Derek yelled. "This has nothing to do with my father." He was lying, and Philip knew that. It made Derek angrier, but he bit the anger back, cramming it deeper into his splitting head. Philip didn't say anything for a while; he just sat there on the edge of the tub.

Finally Derek spoke. "Philip?" he asked quietly. "Could you just leave me alone for a little while? Please?"

Philip nodded. "Sure thing, Derek." He stood and turned to leave.

"—And, Philip?" Philip turned back to him. "Don't tell anyone I'm here . . . please?"

Philip smiled gently. "I wasn't planning to." He turned

and left, closing the door quietly behind him, leaving Derek alone in the tub, to deal with The Dragon.

Derek wished he could cry so his anger would drip out of his eyes and down the drain, but he couldn't. He hadn't cried when his father died. He hadn't cried at the funeral, and he couldn't make himself cry in a stupid Russian bathroom, but oh, did he want to.

He wanted to let the tears fly, because he knew no matter how long he waited, his father was not going to give him any of the answers.

THAT NIGHT, in his bedroom, Derek stared out of his window. Looking at the city lights always helped him forget about his aching head. His view just cleared the tops of the trees in the small park across the street—trees that were just beginning to come back to life after the cold Soviet winter. Above the trees, Derek could see the apartment buildings beyond, and the distant lights of Moscow University across the Moscow River.

As he sat there, an idle thought, and a face he had only seen once filled his mind.

Anna Shafiroff.

Now, there was a girl who had been tossed around by the heartless ways of the world—a girl who had seen so much trouble in her life, it made Derek's complaints seem small and insignificant—but still, there was something she and Derek had very much in common.

Like Anna, Derek knew how it felt to be an outsider—fitting absolutely nowhere in the grand scheme of things, then being put in a cage to be forgotten about. Derek was a prisoner of American diplomacy; Anna was a prisoner of Soviet politics, and as Derek thought about it, it seemed to him that being the son of an ambassador wasn't much different from being the daughter of a dissident. A cage was a cage. That his was a golden one didn't make it any less oppressive.

Anna Shafiroff.

Even the sound of her name was comforting. The more Derek concentrated, the more he could picture her face, and it eased his headache the tiniest bit. *If she's a dissident's daughter,* thought Derek, *she must like Americans.*

Derek closed his eyes tightly, as the gentle, smiling image of Anna became clearer in his mind. *I wonder if she could like an American like me?*

What a loaded question *that* was. Somehow, in the tumultuous crowds of Moscow, he would have to find her, and find the answer.

CHAPTER 4

Derek's Great Escape

While the mysterious Anna Shafiroff attended a Soviet school somewhere in Moscow, Derek struggled his way through his first days at the Anglo-American school.

Derek's first week of school was no better than the first day, and he was already counting down the days until school let out for summer.

The workload was fine, his teachers were fine—even his beginning Russian class (Russian-for-Idiots, he called it, since that's how he felt in the class) was fine—but no matter how much he enjoyed his classes, school was no fun with no friends.

When he arrived home from High School Hell on Friday, his mother was *actually* home, by some miraculous feat. She was on her way out, of course.

Standing beside her were Laurel and Hardy.

"These are tailors," said Ambassador Wilder. "They're going to fit you with a tuxedo for your introduction at the Spring Ball next week."

"What?"

Instantly Laurel and Hardy were all over him, jabbering in Russian and sticking their tape measures in places where they were not wanted. Derek, who considered high-tops and new 501 jeans as formal as he got, was not pleased.

"What do you mean 'introduction'?" he asked.

"Didn't Jim tell you? I told Jim to tell you!"

"Big Jim has the mind of a brain-dead cockroach. Of course he didn't tell me."

"Oh. Well, you're going to be officially introduced to the diplomatic community next week. Now you know," his mom said, looking at her watch.

"Do I have to wear a tuxedo?"

"Embassy balls are always black-tie events," she said.

"Fine," said Derek. "Then buy me a black tie, not a tuxedo!" Laurel and Hardy poked and prodded him up and down, like mad scientists building a Frankenstein monster. It must have been a ridiculous sight, since both Svetlana the cook and Harold-the-Gun had run into the living room to watch. His sister was laughing.

"Mom, this is embarrassing. Can't we do this somewhere else?"

"Quiet," she said. "They're almost done."

"I don't even want to be introduced at a stupid ball!" said Derek. "You didn't even ask me if I wanted to!"

"You know what your problem is?" said his mother. "Your problem is that you're always contrary. No matter what anyone says to you, you want to do the opposite. Someone says turn left, you want to turn right. Someone says wear a tuxedo, you want to wear torn jeans."

Derek supposed she was right about that—being contrary had become second nature to him—and more often than not, his attitude screwed things up in the worst way. It was just that he hated being *told* to do something. Perhaps if people asked him, rather than ordered him around, he would be more agreeable, and the world would be a happier place.

"You know what your problem is?" mimicked his sister. "You're a big fat pain in the butt!"

"I thought you liked parties," said Ambassador Wilder.

"I do, but . . ."

"Good!" said his mom, not even listening to him. "Because as the ambassador's son, you're expected to attend all the big events, and I expect you to be a gentleman."

Derek rolled his eyeballs. They had big parties every single week. What a way to go—death by party.

"I know you're going to have a good time at this ball," said Ambassador Wilder, "because I've made special arrangements for all the diplomats and Soviet officials to bring their teenage children—some of your friends from school will be there."

Derek didn't bother to tell her that he didn't have any friends from school.

"I have to go," his mom said, just as the tailors finished their business. "I won't be home for dinner tonight, but I told Svetlana to cook whatever you want. Don't eat before dinner, don't give Svetlana a hard time, and for goodness' sakes, Derek, tie those shoelaces before you break your neck!" At last she turned to go.

Derek sighed. "So long, Mom."

Ambassador Wilder hurried outside, where a limousine awaited to spirit her off.

Typical, thought Derek. *How typical.* He had wanted to tell her about his trials and tribulations at the Anglo-American school, but what was the point? She never really listened anyway. It made him wonder whether or not anything he said or did was important to anyone at all. It made him want to scream and break something, just so someone would notice him—notice that he was more than just a mannequin to be fit for a tuxedo.

"The ambassador's son must look presentable at the ball," said Svetlana, as he entered the kitchen.

"I'm not 'the ambassador's son,' " he answered. "My name is Derek: *D, e, r, e, k.*" Derek grabbed a handful of cookies from the cookie jar and wolfed them down as if to spite his mother. Then he hurried out the front door to get out of that house and away from everyone.

His mother had already left, and the iron gate around the Spaso House grounds had been closed. Derek stood alone inside the gate, peering out. The street before him was filled with people hurrying home from work. For a week Derek had come out to the gates, looked out, and wished he could go and explore. No matter how many parties and feasts his mother planned, one thing would not change. This house was a prison.

"What's the matter today?" Philip asked, coming up behind him.

"She's making me go to all these parties. . . ." As he said it, he realized how stupid it sounded.

"Don't you like parties?" asked Philip.

"Yeah," said Derek. "I also like chocolate ice-cream cones, but I don't like them rammed down my throat with a jackhammer."

Philip got the picture.

"Well, Derek," he said, changing the subject, "I've got some news that might cheer you up."

"Don't tell me," said Derek. "My tuxedo is going to be green with pink polka dots, and I can't do anything about it, because my mother insists, right?"

Philip laughed. "No, nothing like that. It's just that I've finally convinced your mother to send 'Big Jim' back to the embassy. He won't be your bodyguard anymore."

Will wonders never cease! And a big lot of difference it made, too. Now that Derek was in solitary confinement within these gates, his mother had complete control of him; she didn't need Big Jim anymore. A dog inside a fence doesn't need a leash.

Derek gazed through the gate. On the other side were two Soviet guards, keeping Soviet citizens away. The gate wasn't even locked, but Derek was a prisoner all the same.

Philip thought for a moment, then whispered to Derek, "How badly do you want out?"

Derek turned to Philip with his eyes wide. Was Philip actually offering him a chance to get out? Or was he just trying to taunt and tease him?

"I want out of here more than anything in the world!" said Derek. It was clear by the look on Philip's face that he believed Derek. Philip was definitely not the hard dungeonmaster his mother, or Big Jim, was.

"Please!" said Derek. "I'd do anything! And I wouldn't cause any problems. I just want to walk around; you know? Maybe meet some kids, that's all."

"If I let you go this one time, would you be back by six o'clock sharp?"

Derek couldn't believe what he was hearing. "Swear on my life!"

"I don't know why," said Philip, "but I trust you. You have two hours. Go on; I'll cover for you."

Derek was speechless. "You'd do that for me, Philip?"

"I said I would, didn't I? Now get out of here, before we both get caught." Philip opened the gate.

"I won't forget this, Philip! Thanks!" Derek took one step through the gate, and then another, and before long he was racing through the crowds.

DEREK WANDERED aimlessly, listening to the sounds and voices around him, instead of the Discman in his jacket pocket. He had two hours of discovery before him; two hours in which he didn't have to be "the ambassador's son," locked up in the ambassador's house. Two hours of freedom—and who knew what he might find? What a fantastic two hours this was going to be!

Fifteen minutes into Derek's two-hour liberty, something fantastic did happen. As Derek wandered through the streets, he heard the most beautiful, most wondrous sound he had heard since arriving in Moscow. A sound that made his heart leap and lifted his spirits even higher. It was a hollow, dull, *thud-thud-thud* that was unmistakably the sound of a bouncing basketball!

He cocked his head to see where the sound was coming from. *Bang!* He heard the ball hit a backboard. No doubt about it. Someone, somewhere, was playing basketball. Derek raced off toward the sound, hurrying down an alley, and then he heard it again, above him. He looked up to see the huge windows of a school. Of course! Every Soviet school would have basketball courts—and now, without Big Jim on his tail, he might be able to get in.

The wide doorway to the school was ajar, and there were no guards to stop him. Derek found the stairwell, and hurried in the direction of the sound. He ran down a long, dimly lit hallway to a pair of double doors, and pulled them open to reveal a huge gym with two basketball courts, both crowded with Soviet teens playing.

It was like finding water in the desert. Derek stood on the sidelines for a moment, letting the joy of this wondrous discovery sink in. They were playing basketball! He was back in the real world again.

When a boy took a lay-up and missed, the ball bounced out of the court and right into Derek's hands.

"Hey," said Derek, forgetting where he was. "Can I get into your game?"

All heads on the court turned to him. Everyone suddenly froze, as if they had all detected a spy in their midst.

Derek looked around. Even those on the sidelines watched him, and suddenly being the center of attention in this group of foreign kids made him wish he had never come. It made him feel like running all the way to his comfortable home, sitting on his comfortable couch, and watching comfortable American TV. Big Jim wasn't even there to get him out of this. Maybe his mother had been right. Maybe being alone in the streets of Moscow was a dangerous thing. A very dangerous thing.

The Soviets stared at him, examining him; God knew what was in their minds. They were silent, and all Derek could hear were the cars outside, and the beating of his own heart. What if they wanted to fight? Derek was strong, but no match for a Soviet gang. Is that what he had stumbled into? Did they have those here? What would they do to an American?

One of them, a boy who seemed to be sixteen or so,

with dark, wiry hair and thick eyebrows, approached him. Derek swallowed.

"Here," Derek said, handing him back the ball. He didn't take it. "Here," Derek said again. "Your ball." It was obvious that the boy didn't speak English. As Derek looked around, he was certain that none of them did.

The boy with the thick eyebrows looked at Derek a moment longer. Then he pointed at Derek, pointed at himself, and pointed at the backboard.

"Da?" the boy asked.

Derek, not knowing what to say or do, shrugged. The boy nodded and led Derek onto the court for a game of one-on-one. The rest of the Soviets cleared the court for this great competition, nation against nation. Derek took the ball out first.

Within five minutes word had spread throughout the rest of the school that an American was playing a Soviet, and their little half-court game had drawn quite a crowd.

Derek didn't know what score they were playing to; he just went along. At first he was apprehensive, but as soon as he scored his first basket, his worries were gone. The crowd cheered on the Russian boy, as Derek knew they would, but they were good enough sports not to boo Derek.

His opponent had deep piercing eyes, like the statue of Lenin, but he played much better than the statue had. It was a close game all along and finally, when the Soviet sank a basket, making the score twenty to eighteen, all the Soviets cheered loudly, and Derek knew that it was the end of the game. Although he had lost, he felt as if he had won.

Putting the ball down, the Soviet boy, who had

sweated a great deal for his victory, held out his hand for Derek to shake.

"*Spasseebo,*" Derek said, "thank you"—one of the few Russian words Derek knew.

The Soviet boy smiled. "Yeah," he said, with a slight Russian accent. "You're pretty good for an American."

Derek's jaw dropped open, and everyone laughed.

"You speak English!" he said.

Another boy came up to him, one who looked a little bit older.

"Many speak," he said in a heavier accent than the first boy's. "We must learn language in school." He shook Derek's hand. "My name is Grigori," he said, and Derek introduced himself.

The boy with the eyebrows stood back, watching as several others crowded around Derek, practicing their textbook English on a real-life specimen.

"How about you?" Derek asked the boy with the eyebrows, as he went to the sidelines to pick up his jacket. "What's your name . . . ," and he added, ". . . comrade?"

"Fyodor," said the boy with the eyebrows. "My name is Fyodor."

THE GROUP of Soviet teens took Derek to what must have been one of the few Soviet pizza parlors. It was small and dimly lit, and the walls were painted with bright psychedelic swirls that looked like something from an old sixties rerun. The chairs and tables looked like they should have been retired years ago as well. Still, the place was quite different from the typical Soviet cafeteria, which had drab gray walls and a scant menu that listed borscht, beef, borscht, mashed potatoes, borscht, smelly fish, borscht, and, of course, borscht.

The pizza place must have been a popular hangout, for it was filled with Soviet kids of all ages, waiting in line for tables, waiting in line for food, or waiting in line for the one pinball machine. One thing Derek noticed was that there didn't seem to be much mixing of boys and girls.

Derek sat in a corner, surrounded by Grigori, Fyodor, and a whole group of Soviet teens, who seemed just as interested in him as he was in them. Only a few of them knew English. The rest sat and waited for translations.

"Chicago," Derek told them. "That's where I'm from. It's a big city—it has the tallest building in the world—a hundred and ten floors!"

The Soviet kids were impressed.

"I lived in this gigantic apartment with my father," he said, mainly because he knew how small and crowded Soviet apartments were. "But now I live here with my mom. . . . She's a teacher," he lied, afraid of frightening them off with the truth. "She teaches at Moscow University."

And then came the questions. The Soviets wasted no time in pumping Derek for every little detail about life in the United States.

"Is true," asked one boy, "that you have hundreds of types of shoes to choose from?"

"Thousands," answered Derek. "Is it true that you have to line up just to get toilet paper?"

"No," said Grigori, "but when my sister has a date, we have to wait in line to use bathroom!" A few laughed. More laughed at the Russian translation.

A younger boy in the group spoke up. He had dark brown eyes and light brown curly hair. It was the expression on this boy's face that struck Derek. His face looked very serious, as if he were trying to look much older than his twelve years. "To be truthful," he said, "we have to wait in line for most things. No big deal."

"Is true you have giant markets, and you can always get as much food as you want, even when it's out of season?" asked Grigori.

"Yeah, supermarkets, they're called," answered Derek.

"Is true that every family has a car?" asked another.

"Yeah. Most have two."

"Is true that everyone has big color TV?"

"Yeah," said Derek, "and VCRs, and big gigantic stereos, and home computers and microwave ovens, and electric toothbrushes and electric dishwashers—you name it; everyone in America has it!"

Some kids were amazed, others dubious. Fyodor seemed just a little bit annoyed.

"That's fine," said Fyodor, "if all you want out of life are electric dishwashers. Tell me, how about the thousands of people with no homes, who live in American streets; do they have televisions, computers, and dishwashers?"

Derek was caught off guard by that question. He had no quick answer.

"We may not have dishwashers, but in my country," said Fyodor, "the government takes care of its people. We are given a place to live, we are given a job—we do not have to worry."

He leaned back and stared at Derek, as if waiting for Derek's move across an invisible chessboard.

Derek stared right back at him, not backing down. "Yeah, but in *my* country," he said, "people are allowed to take care of themselves. We're free to live anywhere, and do anything we want. We're not stuck with what the government gives us."

Fyodor smiled as he thought about it. Derek could tell that although Fyodor was not impressed by America's riches, he was impressed by Derek's response. "So," he said, "you have solved our problems, yet we have solved yours!"

"Electric *toothbrushes*?" said Grigori incredulously, and everyone broke out laughing. Derek had to admit that somewhere in search of the American Dream, America had gotten a little bit gadget-crazy. He suspected that most Soviets saw America as one huge electric toothbrush. It was too bad they thought that way—but then, most Americans saw the Soviet Union as one huge iron boot. There was clearly more to both countries than that.

The pizzas finally arrived, along with a pitcher of kvass. Derek's small spicy pizza was actually very good, but the kvass was a different story. Everyone had a good laugh watching Derek turn green when he tried it. It tasted awful to Derek, like flat beer mixed with vinegar, and yet this drink was as common as Coke was back home.

There were a few kids who seemed content just to examine Derek's CD player, finding it much more exciting than an electric toothbrush.

"I had heard they exist," said the younger boy with the serious face, "but I had never seen." He took out the CD and looked at it. "It looks like mirror, but plays music! Fantastic."

Derek turned to Fyodor. "I guess it would get lots of rubles on the black market." He waited to see how Fyodor would react. There were probably lots of Fyodors in Moscow. Chances were that this was not the black marketeer he had heard about—especially in light of the patriotism this Fyodor showed. Still, Derek was curious to know.

Fyodor thought for a moment, and asked, "Are you friends with Mitch at the Anglo-American School?"

Ah, thought Derek, *so this* is *the same Fyodor!* He shrugged, not sure what the best answer would be. "Are *you* Mitch's friend?" asked Derek.

Fyodor thought before answering. "He is . . . a business acquaintance. But a friend? No. Him I do not trust."

"I trust him about as far as I could throw him!" said Derek. It was an expression his father had always used, but here everyone looked at him strangely.

"Are you saying, then," asked the serious boy, "that you have very strong arms?"

"No," said Derek, "I mean that I don't trust him at all!"

"Ah! Now I understand."

They asked Derek questions about America for almost an hour, and Derek was more than happy to oblige. Derek seemed to be getting along with them so well, he figured he could ask them anything—but then Derek asked something that changed the mood of the entire group. It was an innocent question, just something that had been on Derek's mind. . . .

"Say," said Derek, "do any of you know Anna Shafiroff? I'd like to meet her."

It was as if someone had dropped a brick on the table. Everyone stared at Derek, then looked away.

"Getting late, yes?" said Grigori. "Dinner soon."

Everyone else agreed, and they began to get up. The ones who remained didn't seem interested in Derek anymore. Fyodor was the only one not disturbed by the mention of Anna Shafiroff.

"Do you wish to sell your CD player?" he asked.

"No," said Derek.

In a few moments Derek didn't hear a word of English—the teens that remained in the pizza parlor spoke Russian to each other and completely ignored

Derek. Derek was amazed that one girl's name could send ice through a crowd of Soviets. He wondered why, and the mystery made him want to meet her even more.

"You should get home," said Fyodor, "but I'm sure we'll see each other again."

Derek took Fyodor's advice and left, wondering whether or not he had just lost all his new Soviet friends. What a stupid thing to have done!

It was almost six, and the twilight was pushing into night. Ahead of him lay endless streets of square gray apartment buildings. He had to find his way home quickly if he wanted to stay out of trouble, and keep his promise to Philip.

"Wait!" said a voice behind him. Derek turned to see the twelve-year-old boy he had met in the restaurant, the boy with the serious expression on his face. He looked around to make sure no one was watching them.

"I can help you, maybe," said the boy.

"Help me how?"

"You wish to meet Anna Shafiroff, yes?"

"Yes!"

"Well, I know where you can meet her."

Derek felt his open mouth fill with the chilly Moscow breeze. Was this kid for real? Why would he help Derek? After what happened in the pizza place, Derek thought no one wanted anything to do with Anna Shafiroff.

"What was your name again?" asked Derek.

The boy's expression got even more solemn. "Americans laugh when I tell my name. I will tell you, but you must promise not to laugh."

Derek nodded.

"My name," said the somber boy, "is Igor."

Derek laughed.

"Just like an American," said Igor, "to break a promise so quickly." That shut Derek up.

"So tell me about Anna Shafiroff."

"OK," said Igor, "but I want something in return."

Derek rolled his eyeballs—he knew what was coming. "Don't tell me," said Derek. "You want my CD player, right?"

"No," said Igor, and he whispered, "I want you to teach me to play American football."

CHAPTER 5

The Embassy Ball

Harold-the-Gun had polished the big Cadillac until you could see the clear reflection of every streetlight in the smooth black curves. It wasn't going anywhere, since the ball was at Spaso House, but nonetheless, it needed to look presentable when all the Soviet foreign ministry officials stepped out to admire it, as they occasionally did. Considering that they would have their children with them, the Cadillac was probably going to be a main attraction.

Upstairs in his room, Derek struggled to get his cummerbund on. His head still ached, as always, but it was only on medium today.

Actually, thought Derek, the dressing-up part wasn't so bad—it was sort of fun. Fancy black clothes, fancy black cars—it was all sort of Hollywood, like they were going to the Academy Awards. It was something he wished his father could have seen.

Derek looked good in his tuxedo. He looked like his

father. The thought was wonderful and terrible at the same time, as most of Derek's thoughts about his father had been lately.

Even his sister looked good tonight, all decked out in a fluffy blue gown that was a miniature imitation of the gown their mother was wearing. Like mother, like daughter. It was so sweet it could make you cry. Or vomit.

"You're going to like this," Derek growled to the mirror as he finished brushing his hair. "You're going to have fun," he commanded, trying his best to believe it. The truth was that all week he had been dreading being "introduced" at the Spring Ball. It was an honor he could live without. He would much rather be out playing basketball with the Soviet kids he had met, but he had promised Philip he'd stay on the grounds of the house after that day, and he had kept his word.

A week had passed since Igor had promised to lead Derek to Anna Shafiroff, but Igor had vanished once Derek told him he was the ambassador's son. He wondered how long those three words were going to screw up his life. He wondered if he would ever see Igor again. Perhaps he had been "neutralized" by the KGB. That's what Big Jim would have said.

"Your bow tie's crooked," said his sister, peeking into Derek's room.

"Nonsense," said his mother. "You look gorgeous."

"Do I look like Dad?" asked Derek.

"You look wonderful," was his mother's response. It wasn't the response he wanted to hear. He straightened his bow tie and tried not to think about it. Instead he concentrated on how good they looked, all dressed up. They all looked like royalty. He gazed at his sister. Yes, she would make a good queen, thought Derek. She'd be the type of queen that the peasants would want to behead! That thought made him smile from ear to ear.

THE INTRODUCTION wasn't so bad. Derek received a round of applause, and he stepped down with his mother to greet everyone.

You are going to have fun, Derek thought again, *aren't you?*

No! came the answer in his head. *You're going to be miserable and die slowly and painfully!*

Ah, shut up! Derek told himself.

There were Soviet officials, and diplomats from the United States as well as from almost every other nation you could name, all with their teenage children, making this early-evening gathering resemble a very fancy wedding.

Ambassador Wilder began to introduce Derek to the guests, whose names flew in one ear and out the other, since there were so many to remember. The only person he remembered was Mrs. Karpovich, a woman with oversized false teeth and something resembling a bowl of fruit on her head. (Sometime later on, Mrs. Karpovich's false teeth did a triple-gainer into the punch bowl. As far as Derek was concerned, this was the highlight of the party.)

His mother had been right; there were some kids from his school there. Fortunately Mitch wasn't one of them—Mitch's father was a professor, not a diplomat. The American kids hung out in a little group and didn't seem too interested in talking to Derek.

"Get in there and mingle," said Philip, nudging Derek with his elbow, and so Derek sauntered over to the American kids and tried to strike up a conversation.

"Hi! How ya doin'?"

"Fine."

"What's up?"

"Nothing."

"Oh. How's school?"

"OK."

"Nice weather, huh?"

"Yeah. See ya. 'Bye."

Derek was batting a thousand with these kids. He wondered whether they were all boring, or just pretending.

Aren't we having fun? thought Derek. *Fun, fun, fun!*

By the buffet table, Derek came across a group of Soviet teens, all sons of government officials. They stood, with glasses of champagne, like a delegation from some adolescent country. They pretended to be their fathers, and chatted in Russian about some very important things.

When Derek approached, they began to speak in English.

"Good evening, Mr. Wilder," one of them said, shaking Derek's hand.

"Ferretti," Derek corrected, trying not to let it get to him.

"So, Mr. Ferretti," asked one of them, "what is your opinion on the demonstrations in Tblisi, and the Georgian independence movement?"

Derek didn't know how to answer that one. His mother had warned him not to make any political statements, lest he should start World War Three. Derek smiled, trying his best to be friendly, and to lighten up the conversation considerably. "Beats the heck out of me, but how about those White Sox? They could make it to the World Series this year!" The junior diplomats looked at each other, and didn't have much to say on that topic.

"Mr. Ferretti," asked another, "what do you think

about Soviet democratization and capitalist enterprise encroaching upon the Eastern Bloc?"

Derek shrugged. "Hey, as long as they don't encroach on *my* block, it doesn't bother me." He chuckled at his own joke, but these three refugees from a wax museum were silent. "Any of you guys play basketball?" asked Derek, hoping to find some common ground for discussion.

They all looked at each other again, and one of them raised an eyebrow, like Mr. Spock.

"No," said Spock, "but perhaps we could arrange to meet for a nice tournament of chess." The others nodded in agreement. "I am almost a grand master, myself!" He stuck his nose high in the air, as if trying to give Derek a good glimpse of his nostril hairs—and he had lots of them.

"Oh," said Derek, "sorry, chess isn't one of my better sports." In fact he didn't even know how to play, and never had had the patience to learn. He wondered if that made him stupid.

"Mr. Ferretti," asked the third Soviet teen, "tell me, what are your opinions on nuclear arms?"

Now *there* was a ten-foot-pole sort of question! Derek thought about it for a few moments. This called for a very clever response. "Nuclear arms?" said Derek, "I think they're great; with nuclear arms, you could bench-press a thousand, maybe two thousand pounds!" Derek laughed long and hard, figuring it was a pretty funny joke. In Chicago, it would have had his friends rolling on the floor. Instead, these Soviet minor-league diplomats looked at each other, mumbled something in Russian, then smiled politely, and walked away. Derek didn't need to know much Russian to know that they had just called him stupid, and shallow.

"See?" said his mother, coming up behind him, "I told you you'd make some friends."

TWENTY MINUTES later Derek stepped out onto the ballroom terrace to escape from the stuffy atmosphere of the ball.

Everyone Derek had met seemed so cold, so plastic, and so "proper." These weren't real people—real people were out in the street, real people had emotions. The kids Derek had met in that odd little pizza parlor—*they* were real.

From the terrace, Derek could see over the Spaso House fence, and out over the city of Moscow. To the left, between a row of high-rise apartment buildings, Derek could make out the dark patch of ground of the Kremlin, and he could see boats traveling along the Moscow River. At night, Moscow looked like it could be any city in the world. The pinpoints of lights knew no language, no politics. They were the same everywhere, and it was comforting. For a moment he pretended he was on his terrace in Chicago, feeling the breeze off Lake Michigan.

He had tried to be charming, disarming, and diplomatic, but he ended up coming off like an idiot. Who knows, maybe they were right. Maybe he *was* stupid and shallow. He wasn't cut out for diplomatic life; he was just a kid from Chicago—he belonged there with his father, and he would have been there if the world hadn't been so screwed. His anger silently began to rage. It was the world's fault. It was everyone's fault!

Unable to stand his monkey suit one moment more, Derek took off his black bow tie and hurled it out into the night . . .

. . . and the night answered with a rock that came whizzing past his ear.

"Huh?" Derek snapped his head to the right, forgetting his anger, and saw someone standing on the other side of the fence, ready to throw another rock. What was this? As if he didn't have enough troubles, now someone was trying to assassinate him with rocks!

But the assailant put down the rock when he saw that he had caught Derek's attention, and he waved instead. It was Igor.

DEREK FOUND it easy to slip out of the ball. After all, it was his house; why shouldn't he be allowed to move freely in it? He was standing by the front gate in less than a minute.

On the other side, Igor was being hassled by the two Soviet guards. But Igor was not easily turned back.

"Hey, Igor!"

At the sight of Derek, the guards, who knew who he was, released Igor. He straightened his coat, and approached the gate.

"What trouble I go through for you!" said Igor. "Your lesson in American football had better be a long one!" Igor came right up to him, and they spoke to each other through the gate.

"What's up?" asked Derek.

"How is your embassy party?" asked Igor.

"Awful!" answered Derek.

"Good," said Igor, "then I have come to rescue you! Do you still want to meet Anna Shafiroff?"

"You bet!" said Derek. He was definitely not expecting that. Igor was actually going to come through for him! All at once Derek's hands began to get cold at the thought of really meeting Anna. What a way to salvage this miserable evening and turn it into something glorious!

"And my football lesson?" asked Igor.

"You got it!"

By now the Soviet guards—who seemed no older than eighteen—had gotten over their initial intimidation, and were advancing on Igor again.

"Good. I'll wait around the corner for ten minutes. Get out if you can!" And then the guards took hold of Igor's arms and pulled him away. Igor shook them off, and walked away by himself. The guards didn't seem angry; they only laughed at the nerve of this twelve-year-old boy.

Derek turned around and looked toward Spaso House. Could he bring himself to leave? Could he disappear from the ball, leaving behind this pompous world of balding diplomats and humorless Soviet teens who talked of nuclear arms and played chess?

If he did skip out, he would be in unimaginable trouble.

Good!

Was meeting Anna Shafiroff worth it?

Yes!

Behind him there was unending boredom, and beyond the gate was an adventure. Choosing between the two was not difficult.

With Igor gone, the Soviet guards eyed Derek suspiciously, and behind him, he heard a familiar voice.

"Always causing problems, hmm, Derek?" It was Big Jim, who had been invited to the ball. "Why don't you go back to the ball, like a good little boy?"

"Sure," said Derek, putting his hands in his pockets and strutting back toward his house.

But Derek never made it back to the house, and five minutes later, when the gates opened to admit a late arrival, no one in Spaso House saw Derek's shadow sneaking out into the street.

CHAPTER 6

Anna Shafiroff

Derek ran with Igor through the cold streets, and then down to a subway station, where they caught a train just as they arrived. Derek tried to catch his breath, but couldn't—the excitement was rushing through his veins, and the fear of being caught made it that much more electrifying. He rode the train, leaving his frustrations and Spaso House far behind.

"So tell me," asked Igor, above the rumble of the Soviet subway, "would your mother, the ambassador, approve of you meeting Anna Shafiroff?"

Derek leaned back against the hard seat. "Definitely not!" And Derek couldn't help smiling. He'd be in so much trouble!

The train came to a stop, and although it wasn't crowded at this time of night, people still fought to be the first to get on, against a current of others fighting to get out. One old woman nearly knocked a man on his rear as she tried to get in before the doors closed. One thing

Derek noticed: the old women in Moscow were tough. Derek could imagine them playing one nasty game of football. The thought brought a smile to his face.

Igor, who never smiled, turned to him and asked, "Why is it that you want to meet Anna Shafiroff?"

Derek shrugged. "I thought she'd be a cool person to meet."

"Do you think she's pretty?"

Derek nodded. "Yeah."

"I think she's pretty, too," said Igor, almost smiling.

Actually there was more to it than her just being pretty. Part of it was just the idea that her father, Yuri, was world-famous—and meeting her was something his friends back home could never do. Still, those weren't the main reasons. Derek imagined Anna as a girl without a friend to confide in—without a soul to trust. Like him. From that brief instant when he saw her on TV, Derek knew she needed someone to talk to. After his miserable failures at school and at his mother's party, Derek would take a train to the far ends of the earth to find someone to talk to—someone who was an outsider wherever they went—someone who could understand how it felt to be so far away from your father you could barely remember his voice.

Derek couldn't help feeling that something wonderful was going to happen that night—and it would make up for all the trouble he was going to get into when he got back to Spaso House.

"This is our stop," said Igor, and with practiced strength, little Igor muscled his way past the linebacker grandmothers, with Derek close behind.

Across the street was the skating rink, their destination. Anna ice-skated every day, but tonight was special—it was Komsomol and Young Pioneer Skate Night.

The Komsomol, the Communist Youth League, was sort of like the Soviet Boy Scouts and Girl Scouts, Derek discovered—only scarier, because kids were just about forced to join. Derek supposed the Komsomol wouldn't even allow a dissident's daughter to slip through its powerful grasp.

"The Komsomol is a good thing," said Igor, who was a Young Pioneer (a Soviet Cub Scout). "It is the first step into the Communist Party."

Derek shuddered at the thought. He wondered what it would be like if all American kids had to join the Young Republicans, or something like that.

"Sort of like brainwashing," mumbled Derek.

"No," said Igor with that oh-so-serious expression on his face. "Our brains are already clean. Yours may be dirty, however."

A few yards away from the entrance to the rink, Fyodor stood in the shadows, selling a little bit of everything to Soviet teens: cassette tapes of American music, books, even American cigarettes—all the things he bought from kids like Mitch.

"Fyodor's the only black marketeer I know," said Igor, "who can get away with selling things at a Komsomol party! Now remember—don't mention a word about Anna Shafiroff to Fyodor."

When Fyodor saw Derek approaching with Igor, he closed up shop and waited until the crowd around him disappeared. Then Fyodor greeted Derek with a big smile and a pat on the back.

"Derek! Comrade!" he said.

Igor, always the serious one, got right to business. "Derek wants to get in," he said. "Could you help him?"

Fyodor shook his head. "Not easy," he said. "Only Komsomol members and Young Pioneers can get in tonight." Fyodor thought for a moment, then said, "I will help you, but if you get caught, you must promise to leave my name out of it."

"You have my word," said Derek, and with that Fyodor reached into his pocket. Like a magician, Fyodor produced a triangle of red material, the traditional scarf that the Young Pioneers always wore. The Komsomol, who were older, rarely wore them in recent years.

Fyodor held the scarf up to Derek. He reached out to grab it, but Fyodor pulled it away, smiling.

"That'll be ten rubles!" he said.

"Five!" said Derek.

"Eight," bargained Fyodor.

"Seven."

"Deal!"

Derek reached deep into his pocket and pulled out seven rubles, as Igor turned away, ashamed to be a party to the selling of a Komsomol scarf.

Then Derek switched jackets with Igor, figuring a full tuxedo would look a bit ridiculous in a skating rink. Igor, on the other hand, was more than happy to wear the tuxedo jacket.

"Very good!" said Fyodor. "Just keep your mouth shut when you get to the guard at the door, and let Igor do the talking. If you're lucky, they'll just pass you through when they see the scarf."

Derek tied the scarf around his neck, thanked Fyodor, and turned with Igor to get into the long line of teens waiting to get into the rink.

THERE WERE hundreds of people skating around the rink tonight, moving in a counterclockwise circle, and in the center, a dozen figure skaters wove in and out, practicing for some competition, or just showing off. One of them was Anna Shafiroff.

"There she is," said Igor, pointing. "In green."

Derek recognized her immediately. Her long black hair spun around as she swirled across the ice, skating with perfect grace. Although she was surrounded by hundreds of people, she seemed very much alone.

"Wow," said Derek, "she's great!"

"Eh," said Igor, "I've seen better. She'll never make the Olympics."

Igor had brought his own skates, and for a few kopecks, Derek was able to rent a pair. Renting those skates was the biggest mistake Derek had made since arriving in the Soviet Union—mainly because Derek couldn't skate if his life, and the lives of everyone he knew, depended on it. Ice hockey was the one sport he had never taken an interest in, so he had never bothered to learn to skate. It only figured that ice hockey was the biggest sport in the Soviet Union.

On the rare occasions when Derek had been coaxed into skating, he would spend most of his time sliding ungracefully across the ice on his rear end. Not a pretty sight. Nevertheless, with Anna Shafiroff only twenty yards away, and only this measly barrier of ice between them, Derek had to risk it.

Igor was on the ice first, and Derek followed, hanging onto Igor's long tuxedo jacket for dear life. Igor pulled Derek across the ice like a train pulling a load of bricks.

"Remember your promise," said Igor, "American football!"

"Don't worry; I won't forget," answered Derek, trying his darnedest to keep from doing his famous butt-skating act and trying not to think of how stupid he probably looked. Ice-skating, Derek concluded, was like walking on water, and he still couldn't figure out how people could do it. It must be something you're born with. Like algebra.

Around the rink they went, following the flow of the crowd, and Derek managed to keep his balance as they spiraled closer toward the center, where Anna was doing leaps and spins and a host of other humanly impossible maneuvers.

Finally Derek was in striking distance.

"Okay, Igor, I think I can handle it alone now," and with that, Derek let go of Igor.

That was Derek's second mistake.

Igor moved away, letting his uncoupled load of bricks come to a complete stop. With his legs as stiff as logs, Derek tried to skate closer to Anna, but he was not very good at controlling where he went. Instead he slid right past her, and back into the crowd of skaters, where he was broadsided by a big Soviet kid, who had a little too much borscht beneath the belt.

In an instant Derek was on the ground, performing the butt ballet across the surface of the ice. As his tuxedo trousers absorbed ice water, he turned to see Anna continuing her figures, not even noticing him as he sat there like a moron fifteen feet away. Derek stood up again, picked up momentum, and skated directly toward her, determined not to glide past her again.

This was another mistake.

You see, Anna was performing a spin, with one leg on the ground and the other in the air.

At waist level.

And Derek was on a collision course with the airborne leg.

In one awful moment, Derek encountered what may have been one of the most painful experiences in the history of the world.

"Aaaah!" he screamed, as Anna's foot caught him

where it counts. Down he went, once more to perform the butt ballet—but the ice was the least of his problems.

"Oh!" cried Anna. *"Isvini pazalusta,"* she said—"I'm so sorry"—and she jabbered other things at him.

Had this been a normal situation, Derek would probably have lain there in pain, and moaned until someone dragged him off the ice, but he was not about to do that now. He wouldn't let himself.

"I'm all right," he lied, clenching his teeth, biting back the pain. "Really, I'm all right."

"Ah!" said Anna. "You're an American!" She was certainly surprised, but there was something else in her voice as well. She seemed . . . annoyed. "What are you doing here? This is for Komsomol only!"

"I'm an honorary member," answered Derek, hissing through his pain. Yes, she was definitely annoyed. Perhaps even disgusted. Still, she helped him to his feet.

"You should watch out," she said, with an accent not unlike Igor's. "If you cannot skate, you should take lessons first, maybe."

"Naah," said Derek, "I can skate fine." And with that, he lost his footing, and took a swan dive onto the ice. If nothing else, it looked much more dramatic and daring than landing on his behind.

"Yes," said Anna, "I see how well you skate."

Derek was not about to let this stop him, no matter how much of an idiot he seemed (and he figured on the idiot scale, this ranked a ten-plus).

He stood up, and held a cold, wet, red hand out to Anna. "Hi," he said, "I'm Derek!"

"And I'm skating," answered Anna. "I wish you would allow me to continue."

"You skate very well," said Derek.

"Not well enough," she answered. "Not yet, anyway." She skated a bit more, but when she saw that Derek was not to be shooed away like some American mosquito, she spoke to him again. "So, Mr. American, don't you have a tour bus to catch or something? Why do you stay here and bother me?"

"Nope," said Derek, wringing out the water from his shirt. "No tour bus. I live here."

Anna continued skating her figures around him. "Maybe, then, you should get home."

Derek sighed. This was not at all how he had expected his first meeting with Anna Shafiroff to be. Getting to know her was obviously not going to be easy.

"Why do you bother me here?" she asked, very coldly and bluntly. "Did someone make you do this? Did someone dare you?"

"I don't understand," said Derek.

"Don't play games," she said. "You know who I am. You came out here and ran into me on purpose, yes?"

"Well," said Derek, "I wasn't expecting to get kicked, if that's what you mean. That part was an accident. But, yeah, I know who you are. You're Anna Shafiroff, aren't you?"

"Ah!" she said. "Now I guess I should wear a sign around my neck, no? If I was in America, you would put me in a zoo, yes?"

"No way," said Derek. "Listen, I only wanted to meet you."

"Well, I don't want to meet you!" And with the swift flick of one foot, Anna skated away at light speed, and was off the ice.

In a moment, Igor, who had been orbiting the two of them at a safe distance, pulled in closer to Derek.

"She kick you good, eh?" asked Igor, smiling for the first time.

"By accident."

"She doesn't like you."

Derek glared at him. "Gee, thanks, Iggy. Now tell me something I *don't* know!" He couldn't quite figure out which was colder, his soaking wet clothes, or Anna Shafiroff.

Derek grabbed onto Igor once more, and pointed toward Anna, who was already taking off her skates. "Follow that Shafiroff!"

"I HAVE nothing to say to you!" Anna said, as she hurried from the skating rink. Alongside her, Derek limped, his bruised body aching from his ordeal on ice.

"Why not? You don't even know me! I'm a nice guy, really!"

"I don't care how nice or not-nice you are. I don't want to talk to you, and that's final!"

Anna turned toward the subway station, and Derek followed. He simple couldn't let her get away now. If he did, he'd have to bury his head in shame for the rest of his existence. He longed for the safety of Chicago, where at least humiliation always came in English.

"Give me one good reason why you won't talk to me?"

"Because I don't like you!"

Anna bolted down into the subway, and Derek followed.

"You don't even know me. Why don't you like me?"

"Because you're an American!"

"Give me one good reason why you can't be friends with an American," Derek demanded as a train pulled up.

Anna glared at him with eyes sterner than the Kremlin guards, or Lenin's statue. "I have enough troubles," she said, "without having an American as a friend. Do you know what it's like to be the daughter of Yuri

Shafiroff? Do you? I'll tell you what it's like! They put me in the news, and my friends think I am not normal. The KGB watches me half the time; if I have an American friend, the KGB will watch me *all* the time! No!" she said coldly and finally. "No, I will not be your friend. I will not, I will not, I will not, and that is that. Good-bye!" With that, she stepped into the train. "I would not be your friend," she said, "even if . . . even if you were the ambassador's son!"

Derek dropped his hands to his side. "I *am* the ambassador's son," he said with a sigh.

The anger flared in Anna's eyes. "Liar!" she said. The doors to the train closed, and the train pulled away from the station, leaving Derek alone on the platform.

This was ultimate humiliation.

This was humiliation squared. This was major rejection, and there was no rock in the world low enough for Derek to crawl under. This was the end of the world. The end of civilization. The end of life as we know it. Derek recalled reading a story about a guy named Oedipus who gouged his eyes out. He must have known Anna Shafiroff.

"I could have told you she doesn't like Americans," said a voice from behind, "and saved you the trouble."

Derek turned to see, of all people, Fyodor, stepping out from the crowds on the platform. As if this humiliation wasn't enough, there had to be a witness!

"I feel like an idiot!" said Derek.

"You look like one!" said Fyodor, laughing, and pointing to the puddle Derek's wet clothes were leaving on the ground. "No, I'm only kidding," he said. "To be truthful, it took great bravery for you to speak to her like you did."

Derek shrugged. At that moment he felt anything but brave. "What are you doing here, anyway?"

Fyodor shrugged. "I need my Komsomol scarf back," he said.

"But I bought it!"

"No," said Fyodor, with a sly smile, "you rented it."

DEREK THOUGHT he'd be in terrible trouble when he returned home. He figured his mother would have sent out the search parties and notified all of Moscow that Derek was missing . . .

. . . but it didn't happen that way. What happened, in its own way, was worse.

When Derek walked up to the gates of Spaso House, the two Soviet guards outside recognized him right away. They looked at each other a bit confused, wondering what he was doing on the wrong side of the fence, but they let him enter without any questions—mainly because they didn't speak English.

Derek walked right to the Grand Ballroom, and as he stood at the threshold of the lavish party, looking out over the crowds of overdressed diplomats and their families, Derek came to a disturbing realization.

They hadn't even noticed he was gone.

His mother was down there, gravely discussing a sunken Soviet submarine with a diplomat who looked like a penguin. Hundreds of people talked, and ate, as if nothing had happened. As if Derek hadn't just humiliated himself on an ice rink. As if his existence didn't matter in the least—or, even worse—as if he didn't exist at all.

Derek stood there for at least a minute, staring at the crowd, feeling like a ghost.

Finally his mother came up to him. She was more concerned about his tuxedo than she was about him.

"Where is your jacket?" she asked. "What is that hideous thing you're wearing?"

Derek suddenly realized he was still wearing Igor's undersized coat. He took it off immediately. She was also quick to notice the huge wet spot on the seat of his pants.

"Look at you!" she chided. "What happened?"

"He wet himself!" Dayna said, loudly enough to make Mrs. Karpovich, who was standing nearby, turn her head around so sharply that she nearly pitched her false teeth right across Derek's strike zone.

Derek ignored his sister and stared right at his mother. "I fell," said Derek, daring to tell her the absolute truth. "I fell while ice-skating halfway across town."

His mother stared him down, as a good ambassador should. "Oh, very funny," she said, not believing him in the least. "You sat in a puddle of punch on someone's chair, didn't you?"

Derek sighed. "Sure, Mom, whatever you say."

"I thought so. Well, we can't have you walking around like that! There are important people here, not to mention the press!"

She put up her hand and called out to Philip, as if she were hailing a taxi. Philip hopped up to them.

"You called?"

"Philip," said Ambassador Wilder, "could you do us an incredible favor? Could you lend Derek a spare pair of tuxedo trousers? Give him a jacket, too."

"Why don't you start by telling me where you were?" asked Philip as they opened the door to his apartment, near the rear of Spaso House. His tone was on the verge of being angry.

"Amazing," said Derek. "Somebody noticed I was gone!"

Inside the apartment, Philip rummaged through his closet and pulled out a pair of black pants for Derek.

"So, where were you?"

"Meeting someone."

"Who?"

"A girl."

"What girl?"

"Just a girl I wanted to meet." Derek wasn't going to tell him it was Anna Shafiroff. He wouldn't tell anybody that!

Derek tried on the pants. They fit his waist because Philip was thin, but the pants were way too long.

"So what happened when you met this girl?" asked Philip. He no longer seemed angry, only curious.

Derek looked away. "She kicked me in the nuts."

Philip stared at Derek with a mixture of concern and humor. "Well," he said, "that will teach you not to leave an embassy party!" Philip tossed Derek the jacket, which was too long in the arms, then he knelt down to cuff Derek's pants. No matter what he did, nothing made them fit.

Derek looked at himself in the mirror. The outfit looked ridiculous. Who was he trying to kid? He was no diplomat.

"You know what?" said Derek, thinking out loud, "I hate this country! I hate everything about it! I hate the way people yell at you in Russian, I hate borscht, I hate the stupid reusable glasses they have at vending machines, and most of all I hate the Soviets! Every one of them!"

Philip smiled. "She rejected you pretty bad, huh?"

"Oh, shut up!" said Derek, but Philip only smiled.

CHAPTER 7

Borschtball

The last days of April melted what little ice still hid in the dark corners of Moscow. In the courtyards of the Soviet apartment buildings, kids had long since abandoned playing ice hockey as their makeshift rinks turned into shallow pools of water.

In front of Spaso House, the gardener had begun to revive the front lawn and tend to the flower garden that bordered it. Derek could see this from his window. He could also see the frantic pace of the city street beyond but, as always, that was beyond his reach. His mother was quick to tell him to keep off the grass, so even the front lawn was off limits.

Anna Shafiroff's cold rejection of Derek wasn't the end of the world, but it sure knocked the wind and the fight out of him for a while.

For a week Derek carried on his days in silence, keeping his thoughts and frustrations to himself—keeping himself busy so he didn't have to think about anything. He would come home "like a good little boy" and do his homework, then go out to the paddle-tennis court in the backyard and dribble his basketball alone until dinner. He would eat quietly, then watch videos and do sit-ups until he was so completely exhausted, he fell right into a long dreamless sleep.

His mother was more than happy about this. She finally got just what she wanted—"the ambassador's son"—a robot that did what he was told. A pretty picture of an American boy.

She didn't know anything about him. She didn't know what he felt inside—her career left her no time to care. Her world only had room for caring as long as it could be scheduled in her appointment book. Derek wondered if she had always been that way. Derek wondered if that was what he deserved.

Even Philip was more concerned about Derek than his mom was. Philip would often come into Derek's room while he was doing his homework and ask Derek how he was feeling, how his headaches were, and how school was. Derek would brush him off with quick answers.

"If there's something the matter, it's not good to hold it in," Philip would say. "Hold it in for too long, and you'll explode!"

Derek knew he was right. He knew that someday soon he just might explode, but he didn't want to think about it. "I'm fine, really," Derek would answer, and Philip, who was simply too busy to push any farther, would leave Derek alone.

The truth was that Derek's situation at school hadn't changed. He had given up trying to make friends because it seemed completely useless. He had given up trying to communicate with his mother—that seemed completely useless as well. Derek had even given up trying to talk to his father, who either wasn't there, or wasn't listening.

That week seemed to drag on for a month, and during that time, Igor and Fyodor were the only two people who made life bearable.

Igor would come to the fence after school, asking him about the football lesson he had promised.

"A deal's a deal," Igor would say. "It's not my fault she hates you!" Although Igor was only twelve, Derek was glad to have him as a friend.

Fyodor, on the other hand, never came by, but he always seemed to be around. Derek would see him after school, hanging out with Mitch and his little gang, but Fyodor would always leave Mitch to come over to Derek.

Fyodor was the first one to offer any advice on Anna Shafiroff. "Forget her!" he said. "She's trouble! Besides, there's plenty of squid in the sea."

Derek had laughed, and had taken Fyodor's advice. Moscow was a big city, and Derek never had to see Anna Shafiroff again, if he didn't want to.

ON FRIDAY afternoon Derek asked Philip for a very special favor.

"What would you say," asked Derek, "if I asked to be let outside the gate today?"

Philip, who was busy with some sort of paperwork for Derek's mother, didn't even look up.

"I would ask you 'What for?' " said Philip.

"And what if I told you it was to visit a friend of mine from school, in the American apartments behind the embassy?"

"Then I would ask you if your homework was done."

"What if I said it was?"

"Then I would probably give you permission and have Harold drive you there and back."

Derek smiled. That had been remarkably easy. Derek was about to run out and get Harold-the-Gun, but he stopped in midstep on his way out of Philip's quarters. He couldn't do this in good conscience. Not to Philip. Derek turned back to Philip and stood there a moment before speaking.

"What if I told you I was lying?" said Derek. For the first time, Philip turned to him, not at all expecting this. "What if I told you," continued Derek, "that I was really going out to meet a Soviet friend of mine who I promised a lesson in football?"

Philip looked at Derek, then turned back to his paperwork.

"I can't quite hear you," said Philip. "Next time speak a little louder. Go get Harold."

THE AMERICAN ghetto, as it was sometimes called, was located just behind the embassy, surrounded by a red brick wall, and had Soviet guards at every entrance. It wasn't what you would imagine a ghetto to be like. The apartment buildings inside were very nice, by Soviet, and even American, standards. It was a ghetto simply because it was the place set aside for Americans to live. Americans were free to come and go, but Soviets were kept out. It was almost like a prison, but the two nations could never agree on which side of the wall lay the prison. Derek guessed that was what made Americans Americans, and Soviets Soviets.

Harold-the-Gun dropped Derek off by the main gate, and Derek went in—but the moment Harold drove away, Derek hurried back out into the streets, and to the nearest subway station, his football bouncing up and down in his backpack.

* * *

"I TAUGHT myself to speak English, did you know that?" said Igor as he and Derek walked toward the athletic field. "They teach us in school, but not fast enough, so I taught myself."

"It must have been hard," said Derek.

Igor nodded. "I started when I was eight. Before I met you, I spent much time at the American hotels, meeting kids, and speaking with them, to practice."

"Do you want to live in America?" asked Derek. "Is that why you learned English?"

"No," answered Igor, "I want to stay here in Moscow. I have cousins who moved to a city called Brooklyn, America, but I wish to stay here with my friends. I have many friends." Igor thought for a moment, and the expression on his face, as serious as it was, got even more solemn.

"I am going to be very important someday," said Igor, "and to be important, you must speak many languages, and you must befriend many people—even Americans. I will be in the Communist Party, and I will rise through the ranks. My father is an important man with the Soviet railroads, so I will start that way. I will work my way up through the Ministry of Transportation, then I will become a district party leader, and finally General Secretary of the Party." He sounded as if he were certain it would happen. Igor hesitated for a moment, then he added, "I will be the first Jewish General Secretary of the Soviet Union, and I will finally make the Soviet Union a nice place to be for Jews, so they won't all want to run away to places like Brooklyn, America."

"Wow!" said Derek. It was a pretty intense dream for a twelve-year-old, but there was a sense of naïveté about it too. Derek wondered whether such a thing could ever happen. "Isn't it difficult for Jews to even get into the Party?" Derek asked.

"Yes," said Igor, quite seriously, "but everybody likes me, and even now I am starting to meet the right people who can help me. As long as everyone likes me, and I show what a good Communist I am, I will succeed."

"Well, then, if that's what you want, I'll be rooting for you." Derek thought for a moment, then he added, "You know I'm almost Jewish myself—I'm Italian."

Igor turned to him, thinking he meant it as a joke. Actually, Derek was serious. He guessed you had to come from an American city to know how being Italian could be almost like being Jewish. It had a lot to do with grandmothers who liked to cook.

In a moment, though, Derek realized he was wrong. Being Italian in the United States was definitely not like being Jewish in the Soviet Union. It was a stupid thing for him to say. Stupid and shallow.

Derek looked up to see that they had arrived at a huge athletic field filled with people playing soccer and running around the track. Igor led Derek to a far corner, where he found himself face-to-face with forty twelve-year-olds, all smiling ear-to-ear.

"I hope you don't mind," said Igor, "but I've invited a few friends to share in our lesson."

Derek had to laugh.

WITH IGOR as translator, Derek tried to teach the mob of Soviet kids to play football, but this proved to be next to impossible for several very good reasons.

First of all, football is a complicated game.

Second, Derek was a lousy teacher.

And finally, Igor was an awful translator.

The little scrimmage that resulted bore not even the remotest resemblance to football. In fact, their game seemed to be what you might get if you mixed rugby, soccer, volleyball, then added a third team, and blindfolded everyone. It was a mess, it was confusing, but, most of all, it was great fun.

Derek gave up trying to teach when he called for a huddle, and a mop-headed little boy named "Huddle" ran up to him, amazed and overjoyed that Derek knew his name!

Derek let them play "borschtball," as he had named their newly invented game, and he did his best to referee. The most amazing thing about it was that the game actually made some sort of sense. Everyone was convinced they had just learned how to play American football, and Derek didn't have the heart to tell them the truth.

They drew a crowd that afternoon, and, before long, older kids began to join in. Even Fyodor—who always seemed to be around—showed up to play.

It was almost twilight when Anna showed up. Derek saw her through the corner of his eye, but pretended not to. Although his heart pole-vaulted itself into his throat, he wouldn't let it show.

Igor, who had played long and hard and was covered with sweat, ran up to Derek.

"Well, well, well," said Igor, "look who's here—Anna Shafiroff! What a coincidence." But it was clear by the look on Igor's face that this was no coincidence at all. He had planned this all along.

This time Derek played it cool. He didn't go anywhere near Anna. In a few minutes Anna came to him instead.

"I heard you would be here today," said Anna. Derek didn't look at her; he just watched the game of borschtball.

"I thought you don't speak to Americans," he said.

"I don't know any," she said, "besides you." She waited for Derek to say something, but he didn't. Now it was his turn to be rude. He would not make a fool of himself again. When Derek turned to her, he stared her straight in the eye. It was impossible to read her emotions, and it made Derek uncomfortable—but he couldn't show it. No matter how many doubts he was feeling inside, he had to keep up this little cold war with her.

"I should apologize for what happened the other night," she said. "There were many things on my mind. . . . I was upset . . . and I didn't know who you were."

"Oh," said Derek, "is that what this is about? You're apologizing just because I'm the ambassador's son?"

"No," said Anna, "I would apologize whoever you were. The fact that you're the ambassador's son is just an added embarrassment to me."

She waited for a moment more. "Anyway, I'm sorry. That's all I came to say." She turned to leave.

Derek should have let her go.

He should have taken Fyodor's advice. Being friendly with her could only lead to trouble, because of who she was, and because of who he was. Derek should have let her go, and would have, if he had any sense, but then again, he thought, what did he have to lose?

"Hey," called Derek, and Anna turned around. "Hey, Anna . . . maybe . . . maybe we could talk to each other sometime?"

She thought for a moment. "Maybe," she finally said, with a face as cold as stone. Then she turned and walked away without looking back.

THAT NIGHT, Derek lay alone in his room, letting his Discman rock him to sleep . . . but sleep was coming late tonight. There were too many thoughts keeping it away. He couldn't get Anna out of his mind.

She had said *maybe*! A few days ago it had been a flat-out "no," but now it was "maybe." And she had even gone out of her way to see him—that meant she must be starting to like him. Or at least hate him a little bit less. It was a beginning.

Derek wondered what she was doing at that very moment—where she lived, and what her room looked like. One thing was certain that whatever her room looked like, it wasn't as large as Derek's, and the furniture was not made of fine antique wood. And she definitely was not listening to a CD player.

All at once Derek felt a twinge of discomfort. There was something about being there in that huge lavish room that bothered him. Something about his closet filled with brand-new clothes from the United States, something about his seven pairs of Nikes and Reeboks; something about his Discman and fifteen compact discs. Derek had never thought about it before, but he sure did have a lot of things!

"We don't have all the '*things*' that you do," Igor had once told Derek, as they watched a mob fighting over a few pairs of imported Bulgarian shoes. "We're not poor, though; no one in Moscow starves; everyone has food, clothes, and an apartment . . . it's just that we don't have all the . . . 'things' that you have."

It was true—it was a city where apartments only cost about twenty-five dollars a month to rent, and a subway ride was five kopecks, less than a dime. It wasn't hard to *live* in the Soviet Union. If living was all you wanted to do.

"It's not as bad as you think," Igor had said, defending his nation's honor. "Just because the stores don't always have what we want, it doesn't mean we can't get it. We get many things *naleva*—under the table. A friend owes us a favor, we owe them . . . or we just trade." Igor had looked around to make sure no one was watching, then he had let Derek in on a little secret. "Don't tell anyone," he whispered, "but I once traded my brother's old navy uniform for three pairs of American jeans, two pairs of Reeboks, and a Bruce Springsteen tape!"

Derek laughed.

"It's terrible!" Igor had said. "Sometimes I think I'm as bad as Fyodor!"

Maybe Igor didn't mind the disparity, but as Derek lay there listening to his Discman in his plush, well-stocked room, he couldn't help feeling lousy about it. It wasn't that he was ashamed for what he had, he was ashamed that he had never appreciated it before. He wondered if that made him a Communist.

Derek turned off his Discman, and took off his earphones. The distant sound of rain filled the silence. Rain, and the hiss of cars driving on the wet pavement. This is what Anna was hearing tonight. This is what Igor and Fyodor were hearing. This is what every teenager in Moscow was hearing. Because none of them had compact disc players to rock them to sleep.

It was amazing to think that there was a whole world of people living happily without them.

CHAPTER 8

Glasnost, on a Sunday Afternoon

Derek's survival in Moscow rested on how smoothly he could slip in and out of the gates of Spaso House without his mother's noticing. That part was easy, since his mother was rarely home, and when she was, she never noticed anything that Derek did, unless it directly involved her.

When Derek brought home an "A" on his first Russian test, his mother finally lifted his little iron curtain, and let him come and go as he pleased—provided she knew where he was at all times, and he checked in every hour on the hour. Derek often wondered whether she was being overprotective, or just trying to make life difficult.

In any case, playing basketball with Soviets and spending time with Anna Shafiroff were definitely not on his mother's list of approved activities—and Derek was an awful liar when it came to telling his mother where he was. He knew he'd never get away with making up a story, but he discovered, much to his pleasure, that although he was an awful liar, he was a fantastic half-truther.

"Where will you be today?" his mother would ask.

"At the school gym," Derek would answer. He didn't tell her whose school, however.

Philip pretty much knew what Derek was up to, but he looked the other way.

Philip didn't know about Anna.

Dissidents and diplomats didn't mix; their children weren't supposed to, either. Derek was no fool, and he knew that not even Philip would look the other way if he knew Anna Shafiroff was in the picture. Anna Shafiroff was simply a secret Derek would have to keep. The way things were going, keeping the secret would be easy enough.

He didn't expect a wild card to be thrown in the deck.

He didn't expect someone to start following him.

Derek noticed it the day after the fateful football game. At first he thought that inexplicable feeling of being watched was just his imagination running away with him, but after a few days, he knew it was more than that. He was being followed, but whoever it was did their job very well—Derek never caught them.

He figured it was either some American spying on him for his mother, or it was the KGB. Either way, it was bad news.

One afternoon, Derek went to Anna's apartment building after school. He waited in the shadows of an alley for her to come home. He didn't know her phone number—or even if she had a phone—and so this was the only way he could get to talk with her. As he stood there waiting, he had that flesh-crawling feeling again, and he knew there was someone behind him in the alley. He turned quickly, just in time to see a flash of fabric disappear around the corner. It spooked him out so much that he went home without even seeing Anna.

He had asked Fyodor about it the next day, and Fyodor just shrugged.

"So?" said Fyodor. "You're probably right; you probably are being followed. So what?"

"But why?"

"Trouble is brewing in the Kremlin," he answered; "talk of purges within the Communist Party. When the Kremlin has troubles, Americans get followed."

"So what should I do?" asked Derek. Fyodor had a great deal of common sense and knew all the ins and outs of Soviet life. His advice was always as good as gold.

"Stay away from Anna Shafiroff," was Fyodor's recommendation. "Trust me. You'll end up in trouble. That's good advice, from one friend to another."

Derek nodded, but both of them knew Derek wouldn't take the advice.

THAT SUNDAY Derek had his first "date" with Anna. It wasn't really a date—Derek didn't know what to call it—but whatever it was, Derek had been looking forward to it from the moment he had asked her and she coolly said, "OK."

On that day, Ambassador Wilder had a brunch with the French, a luncheon with the Soviets, a dinner with war veterans, and an evening reception for a visiting Canadian pianist.

This meant that she would be gone the entire day, and Derek couldn't have been happier. He didn't have to check in every hour, and he had an entire day to spend with Anna, free from having to be "the ambassador's son."

His plans were well thought out. He would leave Spaso House at precisely ten o'clock, go to the main entrance of the American ghetto, sneak out the back entrance, take a subway in one direction, hop off of it at the last minute, and catch the subway in the other direction. That way, he could be sure no one followed him. He would meet Anna at the Park of Economic Achievements at noon. A perfect plan. James Bond could do no better.

He stood in his room that morning admiring his clothes in the mirror, making sure his hair was absolutely perfect, and that the Clearasil was camouflaging the single zit that had reared it ugly head during the night. He even broke open a pack of brand-new blue shoelaces to match his blue shirt. He laced his high-tops loosely, and tucked in the long dangling ends, hoping that, for once, they wouldn't fall out and drag all over the floor, getting all muddy.

He was ready to go when his mother did something she had never done since Derek had been in Moscow. Before she left, she came into his room to say good morning.

"My, my, my, don't *we* look sharp today," she said. "Why are you dressed up so early?"

"I . . . uh . . . I'm going with a friend to . . . to the park."

His mom smiled. "Male or female friend?" she asked. What, was there a neon sign on his forehead that said "DATE" for the whole world to see?

"Yes," admitted Derek, "it's a girl."

"What's her name?"

Derek hesitated, but not long enough to rouse suspicion.

"Annie," said Derek, the master of half-truths.

His mom smiled. "Wonderful," she said. "Why don't we have Harold drive you there?"

"No, Mom, why don't we *not* have Harold drive us there?"

Ambassador Wilder shook her head. "There goes your attitude again—Mr. Contrary!"

The Park of Economic Achievements sat on five hundred acres and was filled with impressive stone pavilions, statues, and fountains. There were exhibits everywhere—a model of Sputnik to the right, a jet plane to the left, all glorifying the progress made by the Soviet Union since the 1917 Revolution. It reminded Derek of the New York World's Fair (which he had passed by on his various trips to the East Coast), but there was one major difference. All that was left of the New York World's Fair were a rusting steel globe and the skeletons of futuristic buildings, slowly crumbling next to Shea Stadium. But this place was alive and crawling with people. It was what the World's Fair must have been like way back in the early sixties, and this was where Anna and Derek spent their first day together.

Anna was more than happy to show him around, and she was a much better guide to Soviet museums than Big Jim had been. Although most of their time was spent waiting in lines for the various exhibits, Derek and Anna had a wonderful time. They managed to find countless things to talk about—from books they had both read (which was none) to movies they had both seen (which was none), to the weather (which was comfortably cool), to their clothes (which were comfortably warm).

"I like talking to you," Anna had said sometime

during the day. "You talk about fun things, light things. . . ."

. . . *Shallow things,* thought Derek. *She likes me because I'm shallow.* Derek tried to shoo that thought away, but it wouldn't go—it just lay there, lurking in the corner of his brain, reminding him that his headache hadn't gone away completely.

When the lines for the exhibits got too long, and their legs got tired, they bought ice-cream bars and sat together on a bench by a large fountain surrounded by gold statues, statues representing each of the fifteen republics of the Soviet Union.

As they sat there, finishing off the ice cream—which was the creamiest Derek had ever tasted—Derek dared to bring up a subject they both had been avoiding all day.

"Tell me about your father," he said.

Anna looked away from him. He was afraid she would change the topic, or, worse, decide it was getting late and suggest it was time to go home. She didn't do either.

"What's to tell?" she mumbled. "He's in Romania, and we're here, and he won't come to us, and we can't go to him. That's all." Derek thought she would end it there, but she had much more to say. "It's very difficult now," said Anna, "because my mother is very ill. She's been ill for a long time, but now they are sure she is going to die soon."

"I'm sorry," said Derek. He had heard it before, but now that he knew Anna, he felt terrible.

"It's all right," said Anna. "I've spent lots of time speaking to my mother about it. She's being very strong, and so I will be strong, too. . . . I only wish my father would come back."

"Is it true," asked Derek, "that the Soviet government will let him come back?"

"Yes, but he won't come."

"Why not?"

"Because he's crazy!" said Anna, with more than a touch of bitterness in her voice. She looked at Derek, then looked down. She seemed to withdraw into her own shell for a moment. "I know why he doesn't come," said Anna. "It's because he won't apologize."

"Huh?"

"Our government has given my father permission to return anytime he chooses, on the one condition that he apologizes for all the things he said and did ten years ago."

Ah! So that explained it. Although Derek wasn't much for world events, he did know a little bit about Shafiroff. He had written and said some pretty bad things about the Soviet government. Nowadays he might have gotten away with some of it, but those had been stricter times. He had been the cause of many demonstrations (which is what the Soviets like to call riots), so he was put in prison. While some dissidents lived out their exile in America, or Paris, Shafiroff had not been so lucky. He had been sent to the impoverished town where he was born, within the iron grip of the Romanian government. His only consolation was that his wife and daughter were allowed to remain in Moscow.

"If my father apologizes, they'll let him back, no questions asked," said Anna. "But my father won't apologize."

"Well, why not?" said Derek, recalling his humiliating apology to Mitch. If he could do it, surely a wise man like Yuri Shafiroff could do it, for the sake of his family. "I mean, sure, it might be embarrassing, but it's only words."

Anna sighed. "To my father, I suppose words are very important."

"More important than you?"

"I suppose so," said Anna.

Derek shook his head. Sometimes adults made things so difficult, when they could be so easy. "I guess you're mad at him, huh?" said Derek.

Anna shrugged. "Yes and no" was all she said.

A group of Young Pioneers ran past them, their red scarves blowing with the cool April breeze. They hurried past the fountain, thrilled by all the exhibits that lay before them.

"You know," said Anna, "I was never a Young Pioneer. They wouldn't let me be one, because of who my father was. But things have changed. I was just able to join the Komsomol, you know, the Communist Youth League."

"Do you like it?" asked Derek.

"Yes and no," answered Anna. "I joined Komsomol," she said, "to prove that I was just like everyone else—that I was not a dissident like my father—but I think my plan backfired. My mother thinks joining Komsomol is disgracing what my father believes in, and everyone else thinks that my being in Komsomol is disgracing the Communist Party. They say I don't believe in Communism, and shouldn't be in Komsomol."

"Do you believe in it?" asked Derek.

Anna turned to him, a bit angry. "Why must everyone always ask me what I believe in? Why must I believe in anything at all right now? Can't I just have some time to think about it first?"

That made perfect sense to Derek. He often wondered what his own beliefs were. Sometimes he felt like he didn't believe in anything at all—although he did suspect a lot of things. He suspected there might be a God. He suspected that the Russians didn't really want to blow up the United States. He suspected that somehow evil people got punished for the things they did, but he wasn't quite sure about anything.

He also suspected he was falling for Anna Shafiroff. He had imagined it from the moment he saw her on TV—but now it was really happening, and *that* was incredible.

Anna took a deep breath, trying to keep her anger away from Derek. "Do you remember that night on the skating rink, when I first met you?" she asked.

Derek nodded. Remember it? He still had nightmares about it!

"That night," continued Anna, "was the first time I went to a Komsomol activity, and no one would skate with me, so I skated by myself. That's why I was so angry that night. You know, sometimes I wish my father never spoke out against the Communist Party. Life would have been so much easier. Then people would treat me normally."

"I sort of know what you mean," said Derek. In a way he did. "Just because my mom's an ambassador and my sister has a high I.Q., everyone expects me to be a superbrain. I'm not stupid or anything—I'm really smart—I get good grades, but it doesn't matter. People treat me like I'm dumb—and when I'm around my mom or my sister, I feel like there's something wrong with me. Like I don't even have a brain."

Derek felt a little embarrassed for having told Anna that. Now she too probably thought he was stupid. "Anyway," he continued, "I know what it's like when everyone treats you differently just because of who your family is. Sometimes I just wish I could be back in the U.S. with my dad. He wasn't a superbrain or anything; he was just a regular guy."

"Why don't you live with your father?" asked Anna. She looked at Derek and then looked away, realizing it was the wrong question to ask.

"My father died a couple of months ago," said Derek.

"I'm so sorry."

"It's OK," said Derek, even though it wasn't OK. It would never be completely OK.

Neither one of them said anything for a while, and Derek glanced at Anna's hand, resting just an inch away from his. He thought about holding her hand, but beat the idea down until it crawled away, whimpering.

"You must miss him a great deal," said Anna.

"No more than you miss your father," answered Derek. After that, neither of them had much else to say. With the ice cream gone, Derek didn't have anything to occupy his mouth and hands when the conversation waned, so he was left to feel awkward and uncomfortable—which is how he always felt whenever he was with a girl and a momentary silence came along. No matter how far away from Chicago he got, some things never changed.

In the silence he gazed out over the golden statues before him, afraid to look at Anna for fear of feeling even more uncomfortable.

He wondered if she actually liked him. Maybe she had accepted his invitation just because she was curious about Americans or—even worse—just to be polite.

"Have you seen Sputnik?" she finally asked.

"No."

"It's this way." She stood, and Derek followed. Did she like him? Derek had no clue, but one thing was certain: if she were to as much as smile at him, it would send Derek into an orbit higher than Sputnik had ever seen!

Ambassador Wilder was silent through most of dinner on the day Gorbachev purged the old-guard communists from the government.

Dayna, on the other hand, couldn't shut up about it. "I saw them," she said, "One hundred cars driving out of the Kremlin."

Their mother just ate her salad, preoccupied by the whole thing.

"Anyway," continued Dayna, "It's not like Stalin's purges, where purging meant you got killed. . . . It's more like they got fired."

Derek moved his lettuce back and forth in the bowl. "So then this is a good thing . . . right?"

"Duh!" said Dayna. "Of course it is!"

Derek thought to ask more questions, but decided not to. He was tired of feeling, and sounding ignorant . . . and wondered whether it was going to be a lifelong affliction. He also wondered if Anna would still like him if she knew how politically dim he really was.

"Mom," he asked, "do you think I'm shallow?"

His mother glanced at him, then returned her attention to her plate.

Dayna, on the other hand, gagged on her food. *"Shallow?"* Dayna said. "Are you shallow? Is a birdbath shallow? Is a wading pool shallow?"

His mother chewed her salad and swallowed. "What makes you ask that, dear?" she said.

"Nothing," said Derek. "I've just been thinking about it lately."

"Shallow?" continued his sister. "Is a *frying pan* shallow? Is a *Petri dish* shallow?"

Ambassador Wilder glared at Dayna, then turned to Derek. "Of course you're not shallow, Derek. You just have different concerns from some other people."

That wasn't a very comforting answer. There was silence for a moment, and Derek turned to his sister. "What's a Petri dish?" he asked.

Dayna rolled her eyeballs. "I rest my case," she said.

Since his day with Anna, Derek had been trying his best to be deep, which he figured was the opposite of shallow. He was certain depth would impress Anna. In his campaign against shallowness, Derek was forcing himself to read every page of the *New York Times* every day, teaching himself to play chess, and he was even reading a book on philosophy that he found in the school library.

Derek had to admit it was all incredibly frustrating. Reading the newspaper was like trying to watch "As the World Turns"—it was filled with continuing stories about unfamiliar people and places. He'd have to read for his whole life just to figure out what was going on in the world. Chess was just as bad, since Igor, Fyodor, and even his sister took great pride in beating him over and over again.

And as for the philosophy book, well, the only thing deep about it was the sleep it sent Derek into, even if he read it during the day. Perhaps "depth" was something you were born with. Like algebra and ice-skating.

"Mom," asked Derek as Svetlana brought out their main course for dinner, "do you think I'm good-looking?"

"Good-looking?" said his sister, nearly choking on her pot roast. "Are *you* good-looking? Is a rat good-looking? Is a chimpanzee good-looking?"

"You are a very attractive young man," said his mother, calmly slicing up her potatoes.

"Is a *lizard* good-looking?" continued his sister. Derek swiftly kicked her under the table, and she swiftly kicked him back.

Derek wanted to believe his mother very badly, but he didn't trust her. Somehow she never sounded sincere about anything she said. She sounded . . . diplomatic—as if she always said whatever was the right thing to say, whether she meant it or not.

When Derek looked at himself in the mirror, he was never quite sure what to think. He had good hair—shiny and dark, but not greasy. He was well built, with strong muscles and a slim waist . . . but, on the other hand, his ears sort of stuck out, and one of his bottom teeth was crooked, and he was not as tall as he would like to be, and then there was that one zit on his face that never went away—it just migrated around his face like a tiny tent of bacterial nomads. Good-looking? He just didn't know.

He often wondered what Anna thought about his looks. And his personality. He wondered how long it would be until she started not liking him again.

"Mom," asked Derek, as Svetlana brought out the cherry pie for dessert, "if I wasn't your son, would you still like me?"

Dayna, his mom, and even Svetlana stared at him when they heard that. There was silence for a moment, and then his sister shook her head.

"Too weird!" she said.

Ambassador Wilder finished her pie before speaking again.

"Derek," she finally asked, "do all these questions have to do with that girl you told me about? Annie?"

"Annie?" squealed Dayna. "There's no Annie at the Anglo-American school!"

Derek's heart hit the floor and bounced back up like

a basketball. "Annie's short for something else, barf-bag!" he said to his sister. And immediately Derek set his brain on "scan," searching through all the faces and names of his school until he found one that could even remotely be shortened into "Annie."

"Annette!" said Derek. "Annie is short for Annette!" What luck! He was saved.

"Annette?" his sister questioned incredulously, "Annette Thugberry? You like Annette Thugberry."

"Yeah," said Derek. "What's wrong with that?"

"Nothing," said his sister, "if you don't mind her mustache."

Their mother smiled in a way she rarely did. "What would I do without the two of you to take my mind off of politics," she said. "I'm glad you have a girlfriend, Derek."

Dayna snickered quietly to herself, and Derek breathed a silent sigh of relief. They believed the lie and, right now, that was all that mattered to Derek. If he had to lie to keep his secret, then he would do it, because Anna was more precious to him than anything else about his life in Moscow.

Deep down, he knew that secret meetings with Anna were dangerous. Their friendship was the type of thing that could turn so many diplomatic heads, Derek would find himself on a plane back to Chicago quicker than you could say "Aleksandr Solzhenitsyn."

Stay away from Anna Shafiroff! Trust me!

Fyodor's words echoed in Derek's mind, but they held no power. Nothing could happen to Derek and Anna. They were invincible together!

Stay away! You'll end up in trouble! Fyodor had said.

But Derek had made his decision.

CHAPTER 9

A Scent of Disaster

On May eleventh, Anna's mother was admitted into the hospital, and this time everyone knew she would not be coming out. Derek had seen Anna several times over the previous two weeks, and he could tell by the look on her face that her mother hadn't been doing very well. It was hard on Anna, no matter how strong she tried to be, and so Derek wanted to do something special for her. He wanted to give her a special gift to cheer her up.

He had spent over an hour picking through the two aisles of the American commissary, racking his brain, thinking of what he could buy for Anna—something "important." He paced through the aisles, hoping some divine spark of an idea would come to him, but none did. The truth was that the American commissary simply didn't sell anything "important."

In the end, Derek gave up and bought her some perfume.

However, that little bottle of perfume never made it to Anna.

DEREK KEPT the perfume in his backpack all day, figuring he would go straight from school to see Anna. It had been a good school day, despite the fact that Annette Thugberry had smiled and batted her eyes at him all day. He should have suspected that—telling his sister something was as good as broadcasting it over Radio Free Europe. Now Annette Thugberry thought Derek liked her, and she had even shaved her mustache to make herself more attractive. Derek still wasn't interested.

It was after school, while Derek was going through his locker, that Mitch began to get hungry.

Mitch often got hungry, and when he did, he had this tendency to stick his hands in other people's backpacks and scrounge around for any munchies his schoolmates might have.

Derek's mind was busy with thoughts of Anna, and so he didn't notice Mitch's oversized hand as it reached into his pack. Mitch didn't find any munchies in Derek's backpack. Instead, he found a little bottle of perfume with a card attached.

"What the hell is this?" said Mitch, loudly enough to draw the attention of a few kids nearby.

Derek saw the perfume in Mitch's hand, but he was cool about it. "It's perfume; what does it look like? Now give it back."

Derek held out his hand and waited, but Mitch was not about to miss an opportunity to pry into someone else's business. Mitch glanced at Derek, and took a look at the card.

That's when Derek panicked. If Mitch read that card,

it was all over! Derek grabbed at the perfume, but Mitch held it out of reach.

"Mellow out, dude," said Mitch, and very casually glanced at the card. "Anna?" he said. "Who the hell is Anna?"

Derek could have died. By now at least ten kids had their eyes on this unfolding little scene. "Just a girl! Give it back!"

Mitch took off the cap, and sniffed it. "Very elegant," he said, completely in control of the situation. "Who is this Anna? Some Russian wench?"

Derek reached for the perfume with both hands, but Mitch held Derek off at arm's length. He just loved to watch Derek squirm. Finally he capped the perfume and tossed it to Derek. Derek caught it carefully, as if it were a bomb.

"If she's Russian, you should have gotten her deodorant instead," said Mitch. A few kids laughed at his crude joke, and Mitch sauntered off like some sort of god. It wasn't until Mitch was gone that Derek began to feel a cool, wet slickness on his hands. Derek looked down to see he was holding an empty perfume bottle. Mitch had done a poor job of capping it, and when Derek caught it, the cap had come off, letting the perfume soak into Derek's skin and drip down his arms toward his elbows.

"Damn!"

Derek tried to wipe it off, but only succeeded in spreading it across the backs of his hands and between his fingers. He took one deep breath and realized why such a little bottle could last for such a long time. The stinging scent of the perfume clawed into his nasal cavities, making his eyes tear. He reeked of it, and no amount of washing could get rid of the smell. It smelled worse than a skunk!

Derek turned a great many heads as he stormed out of the school that day, feeling foolish as he held his breath and tripped over his own shoelaces. Even the kids with colds had their sinuses cleared out by Derek's incredible stench.

The perfume wasn't the only thing that spread through the school that day. There were things worse than odors—there was gossip—and just as the harsh scent of the perfume flowed into every corner of the school, so did the name Anna. Her name wafted in and out of the ears of every student in the Anglo-American school, and it was only a matter of time until someone put two and two together.

ANYONE SPYING on Derek that day would have had no trouble following him. Even after he practically boiled his hands off to kill the stench, he smelled like a Chanel No. Five factory. Still, Derek couldn't let that stop him from seeing Anna.

Mrs. Shafiroff's condition was getting worse each day, and Anna spent all her free time at the hospital. That afternoon, Derek and Anna sat together in a hidden corner of the hospital roof, trying to think of happier things. Derek had made it his sworn duty to help Anna forget about her mom's illness. He was good at making believe bad things didn't exist, having learned the trick from his mom.

Together he and Anna engaged in a very meaningful cultural exchange.

"This is called a Three Musketeers," said Derek, giving Anna a bite of the chocolate bar.

"Mmmm," said Anna. "Let me try another one!"

"OK." Derek reached into his backpack and tore open another bar, giving her half. "This one is a Hundred-Thousand-Dollar Bar."

"Very expensive!" said Anna, as she tried that one as well. "I think I like this one the best!"

They sat there for a moment, their mouths practically glued shut with caramel. Derek tried to talk but couldn't; Anna tried to talk but couldn't, and they both broke out with muffled, chocolate-covered laughter. Derek could never remember having such fun, and from now on, whenever he ate a chocolate bar, he'd always remember this moment. Whenever he smelled perfume, he'd think of it as well. Anna had to be an extraordinary girl; she hadn't said a thing about the smell yet. Perhaps she thought all American boys wore buckets of ladies' perfume.

Anna pointed at his jacket. "Chicago Bulls—are they a football team?"

"No," said Derek, "basketball. My father got me this jacket last year." Derek began to smile as he thought about it. "It was the season's opening game. The Bulls were down by two and there were only five seconds left in the game. My father figured there was no way the Bulls could win, so I made a bet with him. If the Bulls won, he would buy me anything I wanted in the gift shop after the game. If not, I had to wash the car."

"Did they win?" asked Anna.

"I'm getting to that. Michael Jordan gets the ball, he dribbles to the basket, goes for the lay-up, gets fouled, and the basket counts! With time out on the clock, he sinks the foul-shot, and wins the game." Derek grinned proudly, as if it had been him instead of Michael Jordan. "And that's how I got the jacket!"

Anna smiled, and Derek thought about his father. "In the end," said Derek, "we both washed the car together, anyway. We always did."

The smile left Derek's face as he thought about it. Even the car was gone now.

"It's a nice jacket," said Anna. "Your father must have been a very special man."

Derek nodded, and all at once an amazing thought came to him. All that time spent racking his brain to find the right gift for Anna, and it was here, with him all the time. He was wearing it.

"Would you like to try it on?" Derek took off his jacket. The wind on the roof was chilly, but refreshing. Yes, he could do without a jacket. He gave it to Anna, and she tried it on, handling it carefully—as if it were made of fine silk. For a brief instant, as she sat there in the setting sun, feeling the rough fabric of the jacket, she seemed to be . . . almost American.

"It fits you better than it fits me!" said Derek. It was true. He was outgrowing it, but it fit Anna perfectly. "Why don't you keep it?"

Anna snapped her eyes up to him. "Oh, no, I couldn't . . . this jacket means a great deal to you. . . ."

"That's why I want you to have it" was all he said. Anna understood. They stared at each other for a moment. Derek thought he might kiss her, but he didn't.

"Thank you," she said. "It is now as special to me as it is to you." She brushed her hand across it, and raised the cuff of one sleeve to her nose, smelling that godawful perfume. Actually, she seemed to like it, for she smiled as she did so.

But then something changed, as if she remembered something she didn't want to remember. She looked down and carefully brushed a bit of chocolate from the jacket. "I will wear it, and think of you after I leave Moscow."

"What?" That caught Derek entirely by surprise. "Leave? You're not leaving? Why would you want to leave?"

"I *don't* want to," she said. "But I must be sent away.

Right now, I stay with neighbors, but when my mother . . . when my mother is gone, I will be sent to Leningrad, to live with an uncle. I am sure of it."

Derek was speechless.

Anna sighed. "Leningrad is a very beautiful city," she said. "I'm sure I'll be very happy." But she didn't sound happy at all.

"If you have to leave, at least they could send you to your father!"

"They would never do that—it's bad politics. It would take a miracle to change that."

Politics! thought Derek. *Here she is, held a thousand miles away from her father, and she's talking about bad politics.* As far as Derek was concerned, politics was bad news. It was just an excuse for stepping on people—whatever country you're in.

"Well," said Derek, fumbling for something to say, "maybe there'll be a miracle."

Anna shook her head. "We don't believe in miracles."

Without a jacket, Derek felt the chill of the oncoming night, but Anna seemed to be the one who needed to be kept warm. He put his arm around her, holding her tightly. It was the first time he had been this close to her. Perhaps he should have felt awkward, but he didn't—it felt like the right thing to do—the only thing to do. Anna looked down at the jacket he had given her, sadly thinking to herself. . . .

. . . And all at once Derek knew his gift meant nothing.

The jacket wasn't enough. It wasn't what she wanted. She wanted her father back, and she wanted her mother to get well. Those were two things Derek simply could not give her—ever. If Derek had that power, his own father would be alive today.

How Derek wished he could have just stopped time for that moment and kept everything exactly the way it was, so he and Anna could sit up there, the sun never going down, as they exchanged chocolate bars and laughed.

But that moment was already gone. The afternoon ticked on into twilight for Derek and Anna . . . and way below in room 819, the twilight ticked on into night for Anna's mother. Nothing Derek could do would change that.

"No, NO, no, no!" said Igor. "And that's final!"

"Why won't you help?" asked Derek.

"Because I could get in serious trouble, and you could be killed!" yelled Igor.

Derek looked around to make sure that no one was watching. To the left, across the street, was the half-mile-long Kremlin wall, and to the right, the Moscow River. They walked alone along the path at the edge of the river. No one seemed to be listening or following them, but Derek didn't want to take any chances.

"They can't kill me," said Derek. "I've got diplomatic immunity!"

"Oh, yes they can!" whispered Igor. "They can shoot you by accident, if they don't know who you are—and Romanian border guards are trigger-happy!"

Derek tried not to think about that. "It's not like we'll be crossing into the West . . . I mean, Romania *is* a Communist country, isn't it?"

"That doesn't matter! Smuggling *anyone* across *any* border is illegal—and smuggling Anna Shafiroff into Romania is insane!"

"Well," said Derek, "I like living close to the edge."

"But I don't!" Igor put his nose up in the air, and picked up the pace, trying to get away from Derek.

Derek wouldn't let him. There were enough people snubbing him, without his best friend doing it as well.

"Just answer me one question: are there any freight trains through Moscow that go to Romania?"

"How should I know?"

"Your father works for the railroad, right? So you should know—or at least you could find out!"

"No, I won't answer a single question," Igor said, like a stubborn child. He closed his mouth tightly, raised his hands to his lips, locked his mouth, then threw the invisible key over the railing into the Moscow River.

Igor should have known that Derek never gave up. "Don't you think what they're doing to Anna is unfair?" asked Derek.

"The Party moves in mysterious ways," said Igor. "If they've decided to keep her from her father, they have a very good reason for doing it!"

"The Party," said Derek, "is falling apart. It's too busy patching up its own wounds to care about what happens to Anna Shafiroff—but *I* care."

Igor shook his head. "I should never have introduced you to Anna! Fyodor warned me. He told me you'd do something stupid!"

"I'm standing up for my principles," said Derek, pounding his fist against the cold railing. "What's stupid about that?"

"Principles? What principles? You're an American!"

Derek gritted his teeth. That was an inexcusable thing for anyone to say—especially a friend!

"If you weren't twelve," growled Derek, "I'd punch you out for that!"

"Why don't you?" Igor threw his schoolbooks to the ground and turned to Derek with his fists clenched by his side, actually ready for a fight. He was just as angry and stubborn as Derek.

Derek sighed. He wouldn't fight with Igor even if they had been the same age. Derek made it a rule not to fight with friends.

"Forget it, Igor," grumbled Derek. "I'll just ask Fyodor. Maybe he doesn't know as much about the railroads as you do, but at least I can trust him to help me."

Igor's eyes went wide. "Fyodor? Trust?" He laughed in amazement. "Allow me tell you something about Fyodor, because it seems you have been too stupid to figure it out for yourself!"

Igor stared right into Derek's eyes, and told him the truth point-blank. It was like a cannon going off in Derek's face.

"Fyodor works for the KGB," said Igor. "He spies on American kids, particularly on you! He's the one who's been following you! For all I know, he's following you right now."

It took a moment for that to sink into Derek's thick skull. All this time, Fyodor had been pretending to be his friend, just to spy on him. What an idiot Derek had been! And he had gone and told Fyodor about everything he did—everything he thought—everything about Anna. Derek was his own informer! He had told on himself!

It was the last time he would trust anyone. He already knew he couldn't trust the Americans in Moscow. Now the Soviets had blown it, too. Well, he didn't need any of them.

"Fine," said Derek. "Then Anna and I will do it without any help from anybody."

"Why can't you leave well enough alone?" asked Igor. "Why is it so important for you to bring Anna Shafiroff to her father?"

"Because it's the right thing to do!" said Derek, but there was more to it than that. "Because I want Anna to be happy. . . ." but even that wasn't the whole reason. There was more to it—a deeper reason he couldn't put his finger on.

Derek sighed. "I don't know." It was true. He didn't know all the reasons, and he wasn't going to figure them out just then.

Igor looked at Derek for a good long time. Derek could almost hear what he was thinking: *Crazy American. Why did I ever try to be his friend? Derek's so stupid and shallow.*

"Yes," said Igor. "The answer is yes."

"Yes, what?"

"Yes, there *are* freight trains through Moscow that cross over into Romania," said Igor. "A few each week."

CHAPTER 10

Someone Drops a House on Derek

It was a dangerous piece of information Igor gave Derek that day. It was a very simple piece of information, but dangerous, nonetheless. *Yes*, there were trains through Moscow, crossing into Romania. *Yes,* there was the slimmest possibility of getting Anna to her father. *Yes*, it could be done.

Yes.

What a glorious, wonderful, horrible, frightening word that was! Neither Igor nor Derek had said another word about it as they walked along the edge of the Moscow River.

That night, Ambassador Wilder had a small reception for yet another visiting dignitary and, mercifully, neither Derek nor Dayna was invited. While the bigwigs ate their feast in the formal dining room, Derek sat alone in the Knoll Room, clear on the other side of the house, eating his dinner in front of the television. The last thing Derek needed was another of his mother's stuffed-shirt receptions. He had been to at least ten of them already, and they were about as much fun as sitting on thumbtacks for an hour. Tonight, Derek had too much on his aching mind to be forced to sit on thumbtacks as well.

FACT: Fyodor was a KGB informer.

FACT: Anna was going to be sent away.

FACT: There were freight trains to Romania.

He tried not to think about it by concentrating all his efforts on escaping into the familiar videotape he was watching.

"I don't think there's anything in that black bag for me," said the poor girl in the movie—a movie Derek must have seen a hundred times during his childhood. There was a moment of silence in the movie, and in that moment, Derek's thoughts came back to haunt him.

FACT: Fyodor was a KGB informer.

All right. Fine. Derek could deal with that. No matter how much it hurt and no matter how much it added to his anger, he could deal with it. It just reinforced something he learned the moment his parents got divorced: You can't trust anyone. Not your parents, not your friends.

"The only way to get Dorothy back to Kansas is for me to take her there myself!" said Professor Marvel on the TV screen, with a smile.

"Oh, will you?! Could you?! Are you a clever enough Wizard? . . ."

"Child, you cut me to the quick! Why, I'm an old Kansas man myself"—and then Professor Marvel went on to explain how his hot-air balloon went off course and landed him smack in the middle of the Emerald City.

FACT: Anna was going to be sent away.

All right. Fine. Derek could deal with that too. Sure, it would make life painfully unbearable; sure, it would rip his heart in two; sure, it would mean he'd be left alone again, but he could deal with that—it was either deal with it, or crawl under a rock and disappear. He hadn't disappeared when his father died, and he was wise enough to know that he wouldn't disappear if Anna left. Hard though it might be, one way or another, life would go on without Anna.

On the television, crowds of people dressed in green surrounded a weird-looking hot-air balloon that had "Omaha State Fair" written on its side. Derek fast-forwarded past Professor Marvel's long-winded farewell speech, to the point where Toto jumps out of the balloon basket and Professor Marvel takes off into the skies alone.

"Come back!" everyone cried.

"I can't come back," yelled Professor Marvel. *"I don't know how it works!"*

FACT: There were freight trains to Romania.

That was the killer. That was the one thought Derek simply couldn't handle. He had dreamed of being Anna's hero; he dreamed of taking her across the miles of Eastern Europe to her father, but something happened that Derek never expected—Igor said *yes*. *Yes*, there were trains. *Yes*, you could do it if you really wanted to.

Having a dream was one thing, but actually going through with it? That was something else entirely.

It was like dreaming of being a professional basketball player, and then being plopped down with a ball in a crowded arena, surrounded by nine seven-foot-tall bruisers.

It was incredibly scary.

The thought of actually taking Anna to see her father was incredibly scary as well—too scary for Derek to think about right now, so he tried to file the thought away in that part of his brain reserved for headaches and wishes that never came true. Unfortunately, this thought was a big fat bubble that didn't fit anywhere; it just floated back and forth through his head like Glinda, the Good Witch of the North.

The scariest thing about it was that Derek knew it was something he had to do—most definitely for Anna's sake, but for his own as well. For once he would be doing something not because it was contrary, and not because someone expected him to do it, but because it was the right thing to do. He shook his head, and wondered why, when he had finally found a conviction in life, did it have to involve taking on the toughest border-control system on the planet? Professor Marvel's balloon had a better chance of making it back to Kansas.

"The Wizard of Oz?" Dayna asked as she barged into the room. *"You're* watching *The Wizard of Oz?"*

"Shut up," said Derek. "This is the good part."

"What's the matter, wear out your James Bond tapes?" she teased.

"No" answered Derek, "I just don't feel like James Bond today"—which was true in more ways than one.

"You don't need to be helped any longer; you've always had the power to go back to Kansas," said Glinda the good.

Dayna gouged out a fingerful of mashed potatoes from Derek's dinner plate, and poked it into her mouth. Satisfied she had annoyed her brother enough, she turned and left, shaking her head.

"I've got the weirdest brother in the world!" she said. Derek thought that she was probably right.

Once Dayna had left, Derek leaned back and rubbed his eyes to get rid of the sting. Why did he have to ask Igor about the trains? Why did he have to say anything at all? Now he was stuck. He had to go through with it, or wimp out. Even though the chances of making it all the way to Romania were slim at best—even though when Derek was done, he would have trouble of the infinite variety—he would *still* feel like a coward if he didn't try.

"There's no place like home," Dorothy chanted with tears in her eyes. *"There's no place like home . . . there's no place like home"*—and she clicked her ruby slippers together—one, two, three.

Derek couldn't keep his eyes open anymore—his head simply hurt too much—so he leaned back and thought about how wonderful life would be if there really were ruby slippers, and home was a big, happy farm where people loved you and nobody ever died, and there were simple, crystal-clear answers to every single question.

Life wasn't like that, however, and easy answers just didn't exist. Derek knew that nothing in the real world was simple black-and-white. Not even Kansas.

JUST TWO days after Derek watched Dorothy's house come crashing back down into Kansas, the bad news came flying at him across the breakfast table. It was as if someone dropped a house on *him*.

It was Wednesday morning; Derek hadn't seen Anna on Tuesday, but was planning to meet her after school today. Dayna sat across from Derek, quietly munching on her waffles, and their mother sat at the head of the table, behind an issue of the *International Herald Tribune*.

"Poor thing," she mumbled.

"What?" asked Dayna.

"Shafiroff's wife died last night," said Ambassador Wilder. "Says here that the daughter is crushed by the whole thing."

Derek's mouthful of waffles nearly flew out of his mouth. He went pale, and his stomach tied itself into a square knot. Poor Anna. It happened too soon! He knew how she felt. Oh, did he know how she felt! He could feel her grief across the city, and he needed to get to her as soon as possible. It was more important than going to school.

"Mom," said Derek, putting down his fork slowly, "I don't feel well. . . . I think I should stay home today."

She touched the back of her hand to his forehead. "You don't have a fever. . . ."

"It's not a fever," said Derek. "It's my stomach"—which was half true. His stomach did hurt.

"He's lying," said Dayna. "He has a math test today that he doesn't want to take." This was true, but right now math class was the last thing on Derek's mind.

"Derek!" said his mother, believing Dayna as she always did. "You're not a baby anymore! I'm ashamed of you."

The color was beginning to come back to Derek's face—it passed its normal shade of tan, and went right on into red.

"That's not news," growled Derek. "You're always ashamed of me."

His mother gave no answer, and that was what really opened the flood gates. Derek's anger rose in him just as quickly as his face turned borscht-red. *If I weren't her son, would she like me?* Derek knew the real answer to that question. He also knew how he would feel about her if she weren't his mother. It wasn't a pleasant thought.

"It just so happens," growled Derek, "that I have a very good reason for not going to school today!"

His mother then said to him what had become her favorite thing to say to him: absolutely nothing. She treated him as if he didn't exist—as if his thoughts and feelings were completely insignificant. In a moment, Philip came into the room, complaining that Derek's mother would be late for some all-important meeting.

"Mom!" said Derek, trying his best to control his temper. "I have something *very, very important I have to do today*!"

But the angrier he got, the harder his mother's stonewall became. "Have Svetlana give you Pepto-Bismol if you have a sour stomach. You are going to school today—no playing hookey! I will personally make sure that Harold drives you there and that you do not get out of it!"

"But . . ."

"No buts," she said. "I won't hear another word!" And she was right; she *wouldn't* hear another word, even if Derek talked all day long. He doubted his mother had really listened to him once since he arrived in Moscow. She didn't have the time.

"Don't do this, Mom," pleaded Derek. "Don't just walk away like that!" But his mother strode out of the room, looking at her watch, and Philip tagged along behind her like a trained seal.

"You don't understand a thing!" he yelled. "You never did!"

The moment they were gone, Dayna put in her two cents' worth.

"Maybe if you studied more, instead of running around with Annette Thugberry, you'd do better in math," she said, just like a scale model of their mother. Derek couldn't stand that.

"Stuff it!" he said, "I'm sick of you, too, you little snot!"

Dayna was not about to take that abuse—especially from her brother. "You've got problems," she said as she stormed toward the door—but she didn't make it all the way, because Derek had the last word, and it was worse than a slap in the face.

"You know what, Dayna?" he said. "I wish I were an only child."

Dayna reeled around. Derek could see her face was already turning red—not in anger, but in pain. She had been hurt very badly by what he said, because they both knew that in Derek's blind anger, for that one instant in time, he really meant it.

Derek saw the tears well up in her eyes before she turned and ran from the room.

What a godawful thing to say!

What had possessed him to say it? No sister deserved to be hurt that badly—not even Dayna.

Derek tried to get a hold of his anger, but he couldn't. His temper—"the Dragon"—raged with fiery anger. An anger at the world for taking mothers and fathers away from kids like Derek and Anna or—even worse—turning them into ambassadors.

Yes, his sister was right—there *was* something wrong with him: that hateful, evil feeling inside him that he couldn't control. Only Anna could control it. Only with Anna was Derek kind and gentle. Only with her could he be free of it.

At that moment, Derek found the strength to make his decision. Maybe he was only fifteen, but he had a right to do what he felt was right. His mother couldn't stop him—if she did, Derek would never be free of his anger; it would live inside of him for the rest of his life, and *that* was worse than anything that could happen to him on the way to Romania.

Derek made a secret pact with himself before he went off to school that day; whatever else happened, he swore that very soon, he would be on a train with Anna.

CHAPTER 11

Purged!

Even Derek's schoolmates could tell that something was wrong with him. Although they had always been sort of standoffish as far as Derek was concerned, they stayed even farther away from him today. They could see it in his eyes, and the way he talked. Even his teachers looked at him differently.

"You look like you have a chip on your shoulder," one of his teachers commented. *A chip?* thought Derek. *It wasn't a chip; it was the Rock of Gibraltar!*

On this day only an imbecile dare mess with Derek. Only an imbecile like Mitch.

It was always while Derek was at his locker after the last class that Mitch liked to go after Derek. Today was no different. Mitch sauntered down the drab gray hallway and stopped when he saw Derek.

"So, how's your Russian wench?" said Mitch in that supremely rude tone that only he could deliver. He patted Derek on the shoulder, as if that was supposed to be a kind, friendly comment.

"She's not a wench!" Derek snarled, refusing to even look at Mitch. He was not going to get into a fight with Mitch—there were too many important things to do that afternoon, starting with a trip to Anna's house. Unfortunately, Mitch had other plans.

"What was her name again?" asked Mitch. "Anna, was it?"

Derek ignored him, a trick he learned from his mother, although he wasn't quite as good at it.

Mitch smiled. "What was her last name? I forget."

"None of your business," Derek grumbled, slamming his locker and heading toward the exit. Mitch, however, wasn't about to let Derek go without making him squirm.

"Did her last name start with an *S*?" asked Mitch. Derek spun around to see Mitch's smile stretch halfway across the hall. "And did it end with two *f*'s? Hmm?"

Derek could feel his headache grow. Mitch knew! He had found out! Even though there were hundreds of Annas in Moscow, Mitch, of all people, had found out! Now things were really screwed up! The Dragon was flaring inside Derek, but he fought his temper down. If he blew his top now, it could only make things worse. With his teeth clenched, Derek slowly moved toward Mitch, until he was close enough so that no other kids could hear them talk.

"Boy, oh boy!" laughed Mitch. "Anna Shafiroff! Who would have guessed?"

How could he possibly have known? How could he . . . ? "Fyodor!" said Derek.

"No," said Mitch, "it wasn't Fyodor, buddy. You see, I just happened to be at the GUM department store the other day, and what do I see? I see this Chicago Bulls jacket, and I say to myself, hey, that sure does look like

Derek's jacket. And then I smell Chanel No. Five, and I say to myself, hey, that sure *smells* like Derek's jacket, and then the girl turns around, and I see exactly who it is."

Derek could have hit himself. He should have realized that giving her that jacket was like telling the whole world about the two of them. The jacket might as well have had his name on the back. How could he have been so stupid?

"I'll bet," said Mitch, "that your mother the big ambassador-lady would just love to hear about this!"

Derek knew that was coming—he knew exactly how Mitch's seedy little mind worked. Mitch wanted a bribe to keep his mouth shut. The truth was, Derek didn't even care anymore if his mother found out about him and Anna—but she couldn't find out *now*! It would destroy any plans Derek had of bringing Anna to her father.

"Of course," said Mitch, "I could be convinced to keep quiet about the whole thing."

Just as Derek had predicted. "And what do you want?" asked Derek.

Mitch raised his eyebrows, and pointed at Derek's backpack. "We could start with that Discman CD player of yours."

What a lowlife! Derek was not about to part with his father's last gift to him. He wouldn't give it to Mitch if Mitch were the last subhumanoid on earth.

"I don't negotiate with terrorists," snarled Derek.

Mitch smiled kindly. "Have it your way," he said, and then he yelled so that everyone in the hallway could hear him. "Hey, everybody, did you hear that Derek Ferretti has been dating Anna Sha—"

He never finished. Anything Mitch had to say was blown out of his mind by a strategic fist to the face.

It was by far the nastiest punch Derek had ever delivered. A fistful of explosive anger flew full-force into the face of adversity, and instantly broke Mitch's nose.

One punch was all it took to create instant chaos. Mitch began to scream, holding his bloody nose, which was already dripping onto his precious Notre Dame jacket. People ran out to see what was causing this commotion, as Mitch bounced back and forth across the hall, like a pinball, blinded by the pain. Right now Mitch's evil little mind was far, far away from thoughts of Anna Shafiroff, and if Derek was lucky, it wouldn't come back.

Derek turned to leave in triumph, but his triumph was wiped out as the principal grabbed his wrist in a death grip.

"You're not going anywhere, Wilder," said the principal.

"Ferretti!" snarled Derek, who quickly understood that this nightmarish day was not coming to an end. It was only beginning.

"Where do you get off hitting someone like that?" screamed his mother, as they stood in the Knoll Room. The principal had called and told her exactly what happened, asking her to come to school immediately to take care of Derek. Of course she didn't come—instead, she sent Philip, who had completely given up on Derek and wouldn't even talk to him on the way home.

The moment Derek walked in the door, his mother was on him, dragging him into the Knoll Room for the scolding of his life. She paced back and forth, her heels clicking on the wooden floor. The high-shouldered black gown she wore made her seem sharper and angrier than she already was. She looked like a black widow spider, and was just as venomous.

"How could you do that?" she demanded.

"I had my reasons!" Derek screamed back at her. "He deserved it!"

"I don't care what he did or said to you, you never hit a classmate. You are the ambassador's son and . . ."

"Shove it!" said Derek, "I've had it up to *here* with being the ambassador's son."

"Lower your voice!" she growled. "We have very important guests in the dining room, and you are not going to embarrass me again!"

Derek put his hands to his head, as if trying to keep it from splitting in half.

"Mom," said Derek, changing his tone, trying his best to be honest and sincere, "listen, there are things going on that you don't know about! I have to go out and . . ."

"Go out?" she yelled. "You're not going anywhere. You are grounded until further notice! Do I make myself clear?"

"Mom," pleaded Derek, "you don't understand how important . . ."

"I don't have time for your games!"

"This is no game. Will you listen to me?!"

"You get upstairs and get dressed for dinner . . ."

"What will it take for you to listen to me?"

". . . and come down to the dining room and sit without saying a single word. Is that clear?"

That was when Derek cracked.

"Mom," he said, "I'll tell you everything! I'll tell you all about what's going on, I'll spill it all out to you"—he took a deep breath—"if you can just, *for once*, listen to me! Please!"

If his mother had stopped for just a moment, and actually listened, he would have told her all about Anna, and all about the train and everything. He would have spilled out every secret he had ever held from her, if only she would listen to him.

She hesitated for a moment—almost giving in to the mother in her—almost giving Derek that one second of her time he so desperately needed. But Svetlana poked her head in the door.

"Dinner is ready, Miss Wilder," she said. "Shall I serve, or will the guests be waiting for you?"

She turned back to Derek. "You have no idea how important these next few months are . . . and you have no idea how difficult my job is now." She quickly became her stern, businesslike self. "We'll discuss this later," she said with guillotine sharpness. "Get upstairs and get dressed for dinner."

"No, we'll discuss this now!" Derek screamed desperately.

"I will not hear it! This is not the time nor place!"

"Mom . . ."

She turned to leave the room.

"Mom, don't do this to me! Don't walk out! Not now—not this time!" And then he said the only thing he knew could make her turn back to him.

"My father would have listened!"

She stopped short and spun to look at him once more—but not to listen. Instead she stared at him for a brief instant and said just those words that would grind Derek into the ground.

"Your father?" she said. "If your father were alive, he'd be ashamed of the way you're acting."

With that, she turned and marched out without looking back.

That was it, the last straw. It was the last time she would treat him like that—the last time she would have the chance. Deep down, Derek could feel the anger bubbling up, the chains snapping. She would not crush him again, making him feel that everything he ever felt, thought, or did was unimportant or shameful. She would not do it to him again!

The chains that had been holding back his anger blew apart in an explosion the likes of which Derek had never imagined. Everything went white, and he could almost feel the windows rattle with his anger. In a moment he could hear the glass shattering around him, as a chair flew out of his hands and through the tall window. Then another chair—he spun it around and around and hurled it at the second window, bringing it down in ruins. Then a third chair rocketed through the final window. It crashed down with a deafening roar.

When it was done, and Derek turned back to the entrance, he saw his mother standing there wide-eyed, surrounded by her dinner guests and servants, but nobody dared approach him.

Then, just like that single explosive fist Derek had hurled at Mitch, Derek hurled something at his mother. It was far worse than a fist; it was the truth—a truth he had held locked away for two months. Now it came screaming out of the silence of the shattered room.

"YOU DIDN'T EVEN COME TO HIS FUNERAL!"

Derek stared her straight in the eye. "HE WAS THERE ALL ALONE—*I* WAS ALL ALONE—AND YOU DIDN'T EVEN COME!"

No one else dared to speak. There was absolute silence, and in that silence a small chunk of glass fell from the window frame and shattered on the ground. Now, in a low growl of a voice, Derek dared to utter words that at that moment seemed more true than any he had ever said.

"I hate you." And with that he grabbed his backpack, walking right past her and out the front door of Spaso House. Not even Philip tried to stop him.

CHAPTER 12

Dissidents

Derek had burst out of his gilded cage of Spaso House in one ferocious explosion, and as he stepped alone through the wrought iron gates onto Sadovoye Ring in the wake of that explosion, it was as though he were walking into a dream.

There was no way to describe what Derek felt the moment he marched through those gates. It was a mixture of everything—pain, sorrow, anger, embarrassment—and yet it was all tied together by a lightning bolt of joy that ran through him. The joy of finally saying all he had to say. The joy of breaking free of a world in which his feelings, thoughts, and opinions meant absolutely nothing.

In some strange way, Derek felt very different. He was no longer Derek Ferretti, "the ambassador's son," or even Derek Ferretti, "the contrary kid"—for he hadn't broken the windows and left Spaso House to be contrary. It was a new life he had stepped into, and as the sounds and faces of Spaso House fell far away behind him, they were replaced by the voices of the street, speaking that strange language he did not understand but had learned to feel very comfortable with.

What was done was done.

It was behind him now, and none of it mattered. All that mattered was Anna Shafiroff, and now, more than ever, Derek was a man with a mission.

Derek's mother probably thought he was just out venting steam, and when he calmed down, he would be back. She was wrong. Soon she would realize that Derek was not coming back that night, or the next. Soon the word would get out that Derek and Anna Shafiroff had both mysteriously vanished—but by the time they figured it out, he and Anna would be far from the city, on a train headed toward Romania.

His mother would then think Derek had run away, but again she would be wrong. Derek wasn't running away—he was running *to* something. To Yuri Shafiroff, a man he had never met but who was now the most important man in Derek's life.

And what would happen to him after he reunited Anna and her father? He didn't know. Perhaps he would become a citizen of the world, living by his wits. Perhaps he would disappear into the cobblestone streets of Eastern Europe. Or perhaps he would turn himself in and face the consequences. But none of that mattered right now. Only Anna mattered. Anna and that train. It was the only part of the future Derek cared about.

Derek ran for miles, through the side streets and back alleys, fearing that if he took the subway, he would be spotted and taken home. An uncanny intuition tingled inside him. Somehow he knew he and Anna would be on that train—simply because it was meant to be. Somehow, he even knew there *was* a train out to Romania that night; he didn't even have to ask Igor—he knew it in his heart.

"THERE IS no train to Romania tonight!" whispered Igor as they stood in the dark courtyard of his apartment building, like spies exchanging microfilm. "There is no train, and that is that. Period! The end!"

Igor scanned through the huge ledger he had "borrowed" from his father. "I've looked at this a dozen times. There is none!"

Derek couldn't believe it. He hadn't come this far to be defeated by a stupid railroad schedule. "There has to be one!" he said.

"Look for yourself," said Igor. "There is only one train coming in tonight, from Kostroma."

"Where is it going?" asked Derek.

"Kiev," said Igor. "It goes to Kiev, and that's it. Now will you let me get this book back to my father before I get in real trouble?"

"Are there any more railroad stations?" asked Derek.

"There are nine stations in Moscow," said Igor, "and my father only works at one of them. What else do you want from me? Blood?"

Derek paced back and forth, trying to come up with some sort of solution. There had to be an answer; there simply had to be. Derek glanced at Anna, who stood against the cold stonewall, in shadows. She wasn't saying much.

Derek had gone to see her before coming to see Igor. He had gone to her apartment, where a handful of people had gathered to mourn for Anna's mother. Anna was a wreck as she spoke to Derek alone in the hallway—until Derek had told her he was taking her to her father.

"What? My father?" she had said. "You mean your

mother has gotten me an exit visa?" she asked, overjoyed. "Your mother has arranged for me to go?"

"No," he had told her, "not my mother—me!"

Anna hadn't quite understood at first.

"My mom doesn't know, Anna," said Derek. "Nobody knows. There's no exit visa. There's just me."

Anna finally understood. She had backed away from him. "What are you talking about?"

"I've been planning it for weeks," said Derek, which was almost true. He told her about his plan, but Anna was still unsure.

"Do you want to be with your father or not?"

"Wait! I need time to think."

"There is *no* time!"

"After the funeral, we can . . ."

"After the funeral, they'll have you on a plane to Leningrad; you know that."

Anna was silent. She did know that.

"Who do you trust, Anna," said Derek, "the people who exiled your father . . . or me?"

When he put it to her that way, Anna had been quick to make her decision. "We'll see if there's a train," she had said.

But now it seemed that this was as far as they would get. There was no train, and if things kept up the way they were, Anna would be home in an hour, as she had told the mourners.

Then an idea came to Derek. It was a slim one, but then this whole mission was built on wire-slim chances.

"When did the last train to Romania leave?"

Igor flipped a page and searched the ledger. "There was one that left at four-thirty today. On time."

Derek glanced at his watch. Nine o'clock already—they had missed it by four-and-a-half hours.

"Wait a second," said Igor. He browsed through the

ledger, thought for a moment, looked up at Derek, then back down at the ledger again, then up at Derek once more—as if he had some information he wasn't sure he wanted to tell him.

"What is it?" asked Derek.

"That four-thirty train you missed stops in Kiev also."

Derek's eyes shone with this glimpse of hope, which only worried Igor. "How long does it stay in Kiev?" asked Derek.

Igor shrugged. "It may just stay for a few minutes . . . but if it picks up a load, it will stay until tomorrow morning."

Derek smiled and threw his head back. "Yes!" he cried. That was it! They'd take tonight's train to Kiev, and hop onto the Romanian freight. No problem!

Igor shook his head, knowing exactly what Derek had in mind. "You can't be sure the train to Romania will still be there—and even if it is, it would take you all night to get to Kiev! You'd have to switch trains in broad daylight. It is crazy! You are sure to get caught!"

"We'll see about that!" said Derek.

Igor slammed his book in frustration. "Why could I have not led a simple life?" he whined. "I could have been a good Young Pioneer. I could have learned French instead of English, and never have met up with a crazy dissident American like you!"

"Dissident?" said Derek.

"That's right, dissident," said Igor. "You don't follow anybody else's rules! You make up your own rules for everything, and drive people like me crazy! You're an American dissident!"

Derek smiled. He didn't know why, but he sort of liked the sound of that. *An American Dissident.* It sounded distinguished in a mischievous kind of way. It was a definite step up from being "contrary."

Igor left quickly and quietly to return his father's ledger before it was missed, leaving Derek and Anna alone. Anna still stood in the corner of the courtyard, her tangled hair falling down over her face.

"Romania is very far away!" said Anna.

"Less than a day by train," said Derek.

Anna took his hand. Derek could feel that her hands were ice-cold. "I wish I could be as relaxed as you are."

Relaxed? thought Derek. *If this was relaxed, he'd hate to see what being anxious was like!*

Anna gazed at Derek, said nothing for a while, then she finally asked him the question of questions. The one Derek was afraid she might ask. "Derek, why are you doing this for me?"

"Well, because it's the right thing to do . . . ," he said, but that wasn't the only reason. Now he knew the other reason, but could he say it? He had never said it to any girl he had ever known.

". . . and because . . . I like you a lot, Anna," he said.

Anna just stared at him.

"I mean . . . a *real* lot . . ." Anna's secretive face gave way to a soft smile, and in an instant, Derek knew she felt the same way about him. This realization didn't send him into orbit like Sputnik, as he had predicted—the moment was much calmer. Perhaps this was what *really* being in love felt like, he thought.

As they stood there together, Derek thought he might kiss her—then the might became a probably, and the probably became a definitely. *Yes.* He was *definitely* sure he would kiss her. Slowly, Derek leaned in toward her, and she leaned toward him . . .

. . . and just as they were about to kiss, they were rudely interrupted.

"Ooh!" said Igor, as he saw the two of them. "Are you two making kisses at each other? Hmm? Kissie

kissie!" Igor smirked as any other twelve-year-old in the world would.

The moment was ruined. Anna backed away and the kiss was lost.

"Let's go!" said Igor. "Our train leaves in an hour. It will take that long to get to the train yard."

Igor carried a bag on his shoulders. "I brought food for us to eat on the way to Kiev."

"Us?" said Derek. "What do you mean, us?"

"I am going with you," said Igor.

"No!" said Derek. "You'll get in trouble, and it's dangerous. You've done more than enough already; we'll be fine."

But Igor had his own plans. "I'll be fine too," he said. "The ledger says that there is a train back from Kiev tomorrow, so I can be back here before dark. My parents are already asleep, so they won't even know I'm gone. Tomorrow they'll think I went off to school early, and stayed late. They won't miss me."

"Igor . . ."

Igor was not about to change his mind. He had his own well-thought-out reasons. "If you two go," explained Igor, "and you get caught between here and Kiev, it will be *my* fault for telling you about the train, and I will feel guilty. But if I get you to Kiev, and you get caught after that, then it will be your own fault for thinking up this stupid idea! This trip should be *your* fault, not mine, so I go with you!"

"But what if we get caught before Kiev?" Derek asked.

Igor shook his head. "Impossible," he said, in all seriousness. "I never get caught." And with that, Igor zipped up his jacket and led the way down the narrow hallway out of the courtyard. "Now we are all dissidents," he said. "I hope you feel guilty!"

CHAPTER 13

The Train Yard

The half-moon peered out from behind a patch of clouds, hitting the empty rails of Moscow's Kiev train yard, on the south end of town. The rails shone in the moonlight—endless rows of blue lines stretching forever in both directions.

The fence that surrounded the huge train yard had warning signs posted everywhere. Derek didn't need to read much Russian to know what they said: **No Trespassing! Keep out!** Indeed, the train yard could have been one in the United States—it looked exactly the same. A wooden fence stretched as far as the eye could see to the left and right, and, like almost every other endless fence in the world, there was, about a quarter-mile down, a gaping hole that nobody had bothered to repair. It looked just wide enough for Derek, Anna, and Igor to squeeze through.

They would be breaking Soviet law, thought Derek, if

they crossed into the train yard. Once they were through, there was no turning back.

Second thoughts began to claw at Derek's back. He could almost hear them whispering in his ear. *Forget it,* they said. *Don't go. Run home and apologize to your mother, and crawl into your room and hide from the world. It's easier that way.*

The tingling in his spine gave him that awful feeling that he was being watched. Derek spun around, but only trees stood behind him.

"What's the matter?" asked Anna, but Derek was too embarrassed to answer her.

"Nothing," he said. The trees rustled with the wind. Even they seemed to be watching him, angrily. Derek shook his head to get rid of that feeling, and led the way through the fence.

Far away, across dozens of empty tracks, were several trains, but most of them seemed to be asleep. Only one was running, and Derek could see the dark diesel engine puffing smoke in the distance. That had to be the train to Kiev. In the darkness Derek could barely make out the rest of it: a black snake that seemed to go on forever.

"Keep low," said Igor. "There are guards!"

Derek took Anna's hand, and the three of them crossed through the train yard, the smell of old wood and grease filling their noses as they walked. Each of them fell more than once, catching their feet between the wooden ties. It was a wonder no one sprained an ankle. The rows of iron rails seemed to stretch on forever—the train was much farther away than it had looked. Still they pressed on, moving quickly and quietly across the tracks. Then all of a sudden they heard someone shout.

"Ei, ti!" someone called on their left.

"Down!" said Derek. Instantly the three of them dropped to the dirt. Had they been spotted? Was it over?

"Zdes nelzya kurit!" shouted the guard in the tower again, and the train's engineer, who was standing alongside his engine smoking a cigarette, answered with a wave of his hand and put out the cigarette. The guard hadn't been talking to them. They were still safe. Derek looked behind him, but now there weren't even trees there to watch him.

When the guard disappeared from the window, Derek, Anna, and Igor raced across four more tracks and hid behind a caboose resting by itself on a track. Here they were well hidden from the tower, and only two tracks away from their train. Now the smell of diesel fuel drowned out the musty smell of the yard around them; it even drowned out the perfume of the Bulls' jacket.

"There are only a few guards," said Igor. "Less than there would be during the day . . . but it is still dangerous!" Igor was right. The guard in the tower was up in his window again, peering down over the train. The conductor stood by the engine, waiting, and a couple of men were inspecting the couplers between the first and second cars. Someone was bound to see them if they just walked right up to the train.

"This way!" said Derek. Careful to avoid hitting his head, he crawled underneath the wheels of the lone caboose. He hoped Moscow didn't have a sudden earthquake—if that stupid caboose started rolling, the three of them would be history in six parts. Derek peered out from beneath the caboose, careful to stay in the shadows. He could see the feet of the engineer and the other two men milling about. Finally, when the engineer stepped back up onto the train and the other two left, Derek figured this was their best chance. He just hoped the guard in that control tower was looking somewhere else.

"Now," said Derek, and the three of them bolted out from under the caboose, across two sets of tracks, and right underneath the train to Kiev.

The three of them scrambled out from underneath once again. Now they were on the far side of the train, in shadows. Not even the guard in the booth could see them. To their left was another train—a rusting, abandoned one—and to their right, the Kiev train. The passage between the two trains was very narrow—like a thin dark hallway, with walls of big black boxcars.

Derek stopped for a moment and tried to catch his breath. He had never been so winded. He wondered if James Bond ever felt that way. Behind them they heard the shuffling of feet, but when they turned they saw nothing.

"Rats," said Igor. "Big ones, by the sound of it." The thought of that alone was enough to get the three of them moving again.

At the front of the train, two workers argued over information on a clipboard. The engine steamed, hiding the kids behind a smoke screen. Before them was the narrow passage between the two trains, and so they took off away from the light, into the darkness of the far end of the train.

Once more the scuffle of rats sounded behind them, but Derek didn't want to think about that. So? There were rats. Big deal. The worst that could happen was that they could all die of rabies, right? He wondered if there was such a thing as rabies in Russia. *Shut up, Derek,* he told himself. *Shut up and run!*

"Look," said Igor, "all the boxcars are locked." And so they were—as they hurried alongside the train, Derek could see that every single boxcar was barred by a heavy iron rod. Derek tried to lift one, only to discover that he couldn't reach it, much less lift it.

"The ladders!" said Anna, pointing to the ladders on the side of the cars, which led to the roofs.

"No way!" said Derek. "Riding on top of a boxcar is too crazy even for me! Besides," he said, "we'll get caught for sure that way! Maybe we'll find one that's open."

Onward they pressed, down the half-mile length of the train, ignoring that shuffling of rats, and searching for an open door.

They never did find an open boxcar, but eventually the boxcars gave way to flatbed railroad cars—at least a dozen of them. Each was covered with bulldozers and cranes and other sorts of heavy construction equipment, clamped down end-to-end. This would have to be their means of escape.

Way behind them, Derek could hear the engine getting louder.

"Nine fifty-five," said Igor, looking at his watch. "Right on time!" Igor began to bite his lip, as he looked up on the flatbed railroad car.

"Igor, you don't have to come, you know," said Derek, realizing Igor was having heavy second thoughts that were, perhaps, even worse than his own.

"If you go, I go," said Igor.

Derek smiled. "Crazy Russian kid!"

Igor smiled as well. "I go first!" he said, and Derek boosted Igor, then Anna, up to the platform.

It was just as Derek was trying to climb up onto the platform himself that he heard rats again.

Only it wasn't rats.

It never had been rats.

Behind him Derek heard a strange sound—a sound

he didn't expect to hear. A sound that was absolutely, positively awful.

It was the sound of applause. One person, somewhere just a few yards away, was applauding very slowly. Derek could have died.

"Very good, Derek," said a voice as the applause stopped. "What a show! Bravo!" Anna and Igor looked at each other, then down at Derek. Igor buried his face in his hands. He and Derek knew who it was. They knew that voice all too well.

THE MOON had run deep behind heavy cloud cover, and the only light came from the control tower, nearly a quarter-mile away. Derek followed the voice to a boxcar on the rusting old train on the next track. He could see a shadow lurking in the dark, gaping doorway. Derek swallowed, trying to force away a nauseated feeling. His plan had capsized, but he wasn't going to show it. He climbed up into the musty darkness of the deserted boxcar to confront his foe face-to-face.

"I'm impressed," said Fyodor, "but I wish you would have asked me to come along. I've never been to Romania; it would probably be fun," he said.

"Cut the garbage, Fyodor," said Derek. "I know all about you and the KGB. You followed us here, and now you're going to turn us in. I might be crazy, but I'm not stupid."

Fyodor had nothing to say about that. "Tell me, is it true you broke all the windows of Spaso House before you left?"

"Just three of them," snarled Derek. "I guess news spreads fast in the KGB." Derek couldn't quite see his face; it was too dark. In the long coat he was wearing, and in the shadows, Fyodor looked like a villain from a

James Bond movie. *Very clever, Mr. Bond*, he could almost hear Fyodor saying.

"I suppose," said Fyodor, "you'll beg me to let you go."

"I have nothing to say to you," Derek said, with bitter resentment in his voice, "after what you did!"

"And just what did I do?"

"You lied to me!" said Derek.

But Fyodor was calm. "I never lied," he said. "I told you I sell things on the black market. That's the truth . . . and as long as I keep the American kids at your school out of trouble, the KGB lets me run my business."

"That stinks!" said Derek, his loud whispers echoing in the empty boxcar. "I trusted you! But you were only my friend because it was your job to be my friend! That really stinks!"

"No!" said Fyodor angrily. "I *followed* you because it was my job to follow you. I was your friend because I *liked* you."

"You expect me to believe anything a spy says?" snapped Derek.

"Spy?" Fyodor laughed. "Spy? And just what do you think you are now? You're worse than a spy! You're going against *my* country, smuggling a Soviet citizen to Romania. Who's the spy, you or me?"

Derek didn't have a quick answer for that one.

"If you must know," said Fyodor, "my job is not to spy on you; it's to keep you out of trouble—almost like a bodyguard. But I guess I did a very poor job, because now you're in trouble ten feet deep! Didn't I warn you? I told you to stay away from Anna Shafiroff! I knew she would make you do something like this!"

"Make me?" Now that made Derek angry. He clenched his fists and raised his voice just a bit too loud.

"She didn't make me do anything! It was my idea!" And with that, Derek tried to force his way past Fyodor. He may have been caught red-handed, but Derek wasn't going out with a whimper. If they wanted to catch the three of them, they'd have to stop the train to do it. Derek faked to the right and drove past Fyodor to the left. Unfortunately, Fyodor had played basketball with Derek and knew all about his famous fake-to-the-right, drive-to-the-left move. Fyodor caught him, and they both fell out of the wide doorway to the hard ground below.

That's when Fyodor did something Derek did not expect at all. He pulled something out of his pocket. Something that bore a frightening resemblance to a gun . . . and he aimed it at Derek.

This was a little much for Derek's overloaded mind to take, so his brain sort of just clicked off for a while, and Derek sat there, frozen, like a rabbit might freeze on a highway. Never had anyone aimed a real gun at Derek. He couldn't even remember having seen one this close. Sure, he saw them on TV and in the movies all the time, but none of them were ever aimed at him.

This isn't happening, he thought to himself. *I'm just a regular kind of kid from Chicago. This isn't happening.* Meanwhile, Fyodor just stood there, holding the gun quietly. He seemed frozen, like Derek.

"What are you going to do with us?" Derek finally asked, expecting the worst.

"I don't know," Fyodor admitted. "This is the first time I've ever arrested anybody."

"I suppose you'll take us down to the Kremlin dungeon and spoon out our eyeballs," said Derek.

"Oh, yes," said Fyodor, "and put bamboo shoots in your fingernails, and ants in your underwear, and spiders up your nose. What kind of people do you think we are?" he asked, annoyed at the very suggestion.

"The type of people who pull guns on friends!"

Fyodor only smiled at that.

Far away, the train engine got louder. Derek thought Fyodor would take control of this situation and call in the two dozen KGB men that were probably hiding in the next boxcar to arrest them . . . but he didn't. Fyodor just stayed put, holding his miserable gun.

"Well, don't just stand there!" said Derek. "Arrest me or shoot me, but don't just stand there."

Fyodor shrugged. "Good idea!" And with that he did something Derek did not expect at all. He took aim at Derek's forehead.

Derek's jaw dropped open and all his words hid in the back of his throat. He froze again, like a rabbit waiting to be hit by a truck.

"Say good-bye, Derek!"

Derek tried to scream but couldn't. His heart heaved once in his chest, the train gave two blasts on its whistle, and Fyodor, with a steady hand, pulled the trigger four times . . .

. . . And Derek was blasted in the face by four squirts of water that dribbled down to his chin.

Fyodor doubled over in laughter. "Ha!" he yelled. "Good joke, yes?"

Derek couldn't say anything. His words were still caught somewhere way down in his throat.

"Did you really think they would trust *me* with a real gun?" said Fyodor. "Ha!"

Derek wiped the water from his face, humiliated. But being humiliated was much better than being dead.

"I think you should know," said Fyodor, still smiling at his little trick, "that I am not the bad guy you think I am. You Americans always like to think *we* are the bad guys—but I have news to tell you: if there are bad guys in the Soviet Union, then there are bad guys in America, too. And since we have good guys here, I suspect you must have them as well."

Derek had to admit that Fyodor was right, and he couldn't be angry at Fyodor anymore, as much as he wanted to be. He wouldn't fight Fyodor for the chance to escape, but maybe he could get something from him. Derek held out his hands as if waiting to be handcuffed.

"Arrest *me*," said Derek. "Arrest me, and take me in—but let Anna and Igor go. Like I said, it was my idea, not theirs. Let them go home . . . we can say . . . we can say you caught me trying to run away from Moscow."

"I can't do that," said Fyodor. "If I report you, I must report all three of you—because they'll figure out the truth anyway."

"What happens if you don't report us?"

Fyodor thought about that one. "If I *do* report you, I'll get a commendation. . . ."

"But what if you *don't* report us?" Fyodor still didn't answer him. The train blew its horn once more, and the engine sound changed, like a car shifting into gear. Derek dared to ask again, "Fyodor, what happens if you don't report us?"

Fyodor scratched his neck and sighed.

"Nothing," said Fyodor. "Nothing happens."

That's all Derek needed to know. Nothing would happen. Fyodor wouldn't get the blame. Nothing would happen . . . unless they got caught in Kiev. . . .

A metallic clang rang out from the car-couplers, as the engine tugged on its mighty load. Derek and Fyodor stared at each other in the faint light. It was all up to Fyodor now. If he played by the rules, he would turn all three of them in . . . but everyone knew that Fyodor played by no one's rules but his own. Just like Derek.

With seconds to spare, Fyodor made his decision.

"Hit me!" said Fyodor.

"What?"

"There's not much time! Hit me in the eye . . . not too hard."

Derek just stood there like an imbecile. Behind him the wheels of the train began to move.

"Do it!"

Derek, still not understanding, swung, and hit Fyodor in the eye, lightly.

"Harder!"

Derek swung again and hit Fyodor's eye just hard enough to bruise it.

"Good," said Fyodor. "I will tell them I tried to stop you as you ran from Spaso House, but you knocked me out. I have no idea where you went, or whom you are with."

Derek was too stunned to even thank him.

"Go, before I change my mind!"

Derek smiled in amazement, and turned to see the train picking up speed. Without a second to lose, Derek raced after it.

"Remember: you owe me the world's biggest favor," Fyodor called after him, "and I will ask for it someday." With that, Fyodor disappeared into the shadows.

Wasting no time, Derek ran, picking up speed, until he matched the speed of the train, and caught up with the car holding Igor and Anna. In a moment the train would be moving too fast; he would have to grab onto the train and swing himself onto the deck in a matter of seconds. It was just like a move he had once done on the parallel bars in gym class, only this time, instead of a soft blue mat to protect his fall, below were the deadly steel wheels of the train.

Trying not to think about it, he grabbed the edge of the platform, swung his legs underneath the train, then swung them up and around, and landed smoothly on the bed of the car. Only after he was safely on the deck did he dare to remember how many times he had fallen to the mat trying to do that in gym class.

Derek found Igor and Anna crouching in the deep iron-toothed scoop of a bulldozer, and he hopped in to join them. They were amazed to see him; they were certain the train would stop any minute and the police would pull them off.

"What happened?" they asked. "You mean we can go? Fyodor's not turning us in? What happened? Tell us! Tell us!"

"He shot me," said Derek, with a shrug, "so I punched him out." And he didn't say another word about it.

CHAPTER 14

Romania by Night

The crowded apartment buildings of Moscow gave way to countryside as the night freight to Kiev began its nine-hour journey. Gone were the broken windows of Spaso House, Mitch's broken nose, Fyodor, and Anna's poor mother. They fell farther behind by the minute. Here in the scoop of a bulldozer on the flatbed of the fourteenth railroad car, Derek, Anna, and Igor shared their own private world. No one could touch them or hurt them as they huddled in the darkness.

It was the first moment of rest Derek had since running from Spaso House, and as he tried to slow his heartbeat down to a normal pace, he realized he could no longer feel his anger. Perhaps he had left the Dragon behind at Spaso House.

Derek could almost imagine his anger like a real dragon chasing him through the night.

Well, it would never catch up with him as long as Derek ran.

"Tell me about your father, Anna," asked Derek, trying to gear his mind up for whatever the next few days had in store.

Anna looked at him as if he were crazy. "You know about my father—where he lives, why they sent him there. . . ."

"No, that's not what I mean. Tell me what he's like. Is he hard and strict like my mom, or is he sort of easy-going? You never even told me what he looks like. What does he look like?"

Anna found that one very hard to answer. "Well," she said, "he has a beard—or he used to. It was brown. Maybe it is gray now. . . ." Anna reached back in her memory. "He has very big hands. I remember when I was a little girl, he used to pick me up in his big hands and hold me in the air. His hands were so big, I was never afraid of falling. He was strict, but kind and gentle." Anna began to grin slightly. "He had a big smile, too—and his eyes—he had wrinkles around them, but not angry or sad wrinkles. They were smiling wrinkles. Perhaps that's why they were always so afraid of him because that smile never left his eyes—no matter what happened to him."

Anna seemed lost in her memories. Derek listened closely, trying to see what she saw. "I remember he would play games with me. He taught me to play chess. We would sit and talk for hours about anything—from why the winters were so cold to why the sky was blue and why the moon didn't fall from the sky."

Derek had to smile. It reminded Derek of his own father, when Derek was small.

"I can't wait to meet him," said Derek.

Anna showed a slim smile. "Neither can I. It's been so long since I've seen him . . . he may not be anything like I remember. It will almost be like meeting him for the first time, he's been in exile for so long."

"Your father has it easy!" Igor told Anna. "When *our* grandparents were living under Stalin—they didn't just exile dissidents; they were killed!"

This was not a pleasant thought. Derek knew all about Stalin's reign of terror, during the forties and fifties. Anyone who disagreed with what Stalin said was taken away by the secret police and never came back. The Stalinist purges left a dark mark on the Soviet Union's history that no one could erase. Just like the mark slavery left on America's history. Derek was just the tiniest bit angry at Igor for bringing such a bad-news topic into their little bulldozer world.

"My grandfather was killed," said Igor. "He would have been happy to be exiled to his hometown."

"How about *your* father?" Anna asked Derek, changing the subject. "What was he like, if you don't mind me asking."

"My father?" Derek didn't have to reach as far back as Anna did. "Well, he looked a lot like me. He had dark hair, sort of turning gray just at the sides. He was tall, but not too tall, and he was thin. He had a good job working for a big advertising agency, and he loved sports. We always went to ball games together, every week. We had season tickets for the Bulls—and the White Sox, too!"

Anna nodded, although Derek was sure she didn't know who the White Sox were or, for that matter, what season tickets were.

"Anyway," said Derek, "maybe he got on my case once in a while when I flaked off at school, but I would deserve it, so it was OK. He was a great dad. The best."

Anna nodded, and turned to Igor, who must have been feeling like the third wheel on a bicycle by now, as he munched on the food he brought along for the journey. "How about your father?" Anna asked Igor. "Is he a good father?"

Igor shrugged. "He's there," said Igor, with a mouth full of food. It was more than either Derek or Anna could say. Derek knew if Igor's father suddenly wasn't there anymore, it wouldn't take long for Igor to realize all the good things about *his* father. Derek knew how that worked.

"See this?" Derek reached into his backpack and pulled out his Sony Discman. At the sight of it, Igor's eyes went wide, as they always did. "My father got me this for my birthday. It was really expensive, but he got it for me anyway because he knew I wanted one." Igor took out his flashlight so he could see it more clearly. The edges were already beaten up from all the use it was getting. "It was the last thing he gave me before he died," said Derek.

That word made Anna look down. She handed the Discman to Igor, who was more than happy to examine it.

"Derek," asked Anna, unable to look at him, "how did . . . well, what happened to your father?"

Derek pursed his lips. No one had dared to ask before. The answer was a simple one. A car accident. Happens everyday to somebody. Just like winning the lottery.

But that wasn't the whole truth.

"He was killed," said Derek. "He was killed by a dragon."

Both Anna and Igor looked at him with that confused I-need-my-Russian-English-dictionary look on their faces. Obviously the word *dragon* was not in their vocabulary. That was OK. Derek didn't want to talk about it anymore.

"That's enough about my father," said Derek. "Let's

keep thinking about yours. What will we do when we get there? What will we say to him? Can I even talk to him? Does he know English?"

"Yes," said Anna. "He knows English, and Russian, and Romanian, and French, and a few more languages. Seven in all. Maybe even more!"

"Wow!" There was a wild thought, seven languages. For Derek the English language was difficult enough. It made him even more excited about meeting Yuri Shafiroff. Surely meeting a man who knew seven languages would give Derek a much clearer view of life. Surely meeting him would somehow solve Derek's endless list of troubles.

Even Igor, who was well on his way to knowing a great number of languages, was impressed. "If I wasn't turning back at Kiev," said Igor, "I'd like to meet him myself."

The train plowed past the country dachas, the summer homes of the wealthier Muscovites, and into a countryside so dark you couldn't tell whether the hills were bare or covered with trees.

Igor, tired of being the third wheel, closed his eyes and tuned out by turning on Derek's Discman, while Derek and Anna stood up into the breeze. It hit their faces coldly at first, but as their skin tightened and got used to the cold, it felt wonderful, almost hypnotic. They stared into the dim shadows of the passing hills. No one could have seen them there in the darkness, even if there had been someone out there.

"It's beautiful," said Anna. The wind and train were so loud, she had to move very close to Derek's ear when she spoke. Derek never realized just how much he liked having someone whisper into his ear.

"Beautiful?" said Derek. "But you can't see anything."

"That's what I mean!" said Anna. "No apartment

buildings, no streetlights, no headlights, no signs. Just the darkness. It's beautiful!" Derek smiled. She could have been staring at a garbage dump, telling him it was beautiful, and he would have agreed with all his heart, as long as she said it right into his ear like that! At that moment in time, the darkness was beautiful, the big black train was beautiful, the ugly green bulldozer was beautiful. Everything in the universe was beautiful.

On an impulse, Derek leaped up to the jagged iron-toothed lip of the bulldozer's scoop and balanced there, leaning slightly into the wind, out over the wide flatbed of the railroad car. "Wa-hoo!" he yelled, like a cowboy on an extremely long, loud horse. No one up front in the engine could see or hear him.

"You're crazy!" screamed Anna, laughing at the same time. Of course he was crazy! Being crazy was the best part of Derek's life!

When he began to lose his balance, Derek leaped from the bulldozer to the flatbed of the railroad car. Anna climbed out, and together they stood next to the bulldozer, each holding on with one hand to keep from blowing off the train and into the beautiful darkness of the night. When they had their fill of the wind, Derek led Anna into the alcove between the tractor wheels of the big bulldozer. The wind didn't hit them there, and they were warm as long as they stayed close to each other.

Protected from the wind once more, the skin on Derek's face began to tingle as it warmed up. Anna spoke, but she still needed to be very, very close to be heard. Derek liked that just fine.

"You are wonderful!" said Anna. "Were you always like this in Chicago?"

Probably not, thought Derek. "Yeah," he said, "you know me, the Crazy American!"

Anna smiled. "Crazy or not, my mother would have liked you very, very much!"

All it took was a single thought of her mother to bring Anna down. Her smile was gone. Derek could see the tears starting to fill her eyes—tears of sadness, but also of anger.

"I can't believe she's gone!" said Anna. "I can't believe I won't walk with her in Gorki Park ever again. I can't believe . . . I can't believe I'll never see her at the market arguing over the price of Mr. Vladim's fish! I can't believe it!"

Derek took her into his arms, which wasn't difficult, considering how close they were. "It's OK," offered Derek. "You're gonna be with your father by tomorrow, and everything will be great!"

But Anna still was not comforted. "How can you know that? How can you know what will happen? How do you know we won't be caught, and even if we're not caught, they could send us back even after we've gotten to Romania—and even if none of that happens, how do you know my father will want me, or even recognize me? How can you know any of this? You don't know what's going to happen any more than I do!"

"I *do* know!" said Derek. That much was true. It wasn't just hope; it was knowledge. Derek was absolutely certain they would make it. Anna would be with her father, and Derek would have the honor of shaking Yuri Shafiroff's big grateful hand.

"I know . . . because it's like . . . destiny."

Anna stared at him with that Russian-English-dictionary look in her eyes again. "What?"

"You know, destiny. Like it was meant to be . . . ," said Derek as he sorted it out in his own mind. "You see, the whole world runs on a plan—sort of like school, you know—and if you're following that plan you do OK. If you don't follow the plan, you flunk out. You get it?"

Anna shook her head. "What about your father and my mother? Was that part of this 'plan' of yours?"

Derek hadn't thought about that. "How should I know?" he said. "All right, so I guess the plan really stinks sometimes—like when you get a pop quiz you weren't ready for, and you screw up your whole grade-point average, you know?"

Anna wouldn't take her eyes off him. She stared at him, and then she laughed. "I have no idea what you're talking about!" Derek laughed too—and then it happened.

Derek didn't even know what came over him. He didn't think about it, he didn't prepare for it, it just happened. He kissed Anna, or Anna kissed him, or perhaps they both kissed each other at the same time, but whatever the case, it was a full-fledged kiss, and neither Derek nor Anna would break it off.

For Derek it was like a system overload, and all these incredibly bizarre things flew through his mind as his supercharged brain began to misfire. He remembered he left his retainer at home and wouldn't be wearing it for quite a while. He remembered that he was in need of a haircut. He wondered if anyone had ever kissed while sitting wedged between the wheels of a green bulldozer before, and, of course, he thought about Sputnik.

Yes, destiny! That was it. Derek had hit the jackpot on that one. For once he had figured something out right. This kiss was meant to be. It was meant to be from the beginning of time, just like the train trip. Just like his running from Spaso House.

As Igor baked his brain with rock music in the scoop, Anna and Derek kissed in the shadows without a word, and when they had kissed enough for one evening, they held each other until they fell asleep, exhausted from the evil, beautiful, disastrous, triumphant day.

Derek dreamed of destiny—of that moment when he would deliver Anna into the hands of her father—of when he would talk to Yuri Shafiroff about things of great importance. It was all meant to be that way. No doubt about it.

And Derek went on thinking that way, right up till the moment he fell off the train.

CHAPTER 15

Derek Gets a Pop Quiz

There are lots of stupid things that go on in the world, from big things like war to little things like zits.

Derek had always thought that most of the stupid things in the world happened to *him* more often than they happened to anyone else.

But the day he woke at sunrise on a speeding Soviet train, Derek knew his life and his luck had changed. Nothing could go wrong, and there would be none of life's grand pop quizzes today. Nothing could have been better. . . . Well, maybe it could have been a bit warmer, but that was it.

Derek tried to move his toes. It was a chore, because they were so cold. Even his best pair of padded high tops couldn't keep out the cold. Derek doubted they would have kept his feet warm even if he had tied the laces.

Derek sat wedged between the heavy tires with Anna, who still slept. He idly thought about those tires. If the bulldozer wasn't tied down properly, and those wheels began to move . . . but that wouldn't happen. They had come too far to be crushed by the wheels of a bulldozer!

The hills and valleys rushed by, filled with the long shadows of dawn and trees of every imaginable shade of green and red. Not a house could be seen, not a soul. The Soviet countryside was like another world!

Now that he was no longer hidden by the dark night, Derek realized it was time to take cover in the scoop, so he stood and stretched, preparing to join Igor. He turned to wake Anna, but decided to have a look around first. Perhaps in daylight there was a safer place to hide than the scoop—under the bulldozer, perhaps.

Derek took one step.

That was all it took.

There are a lot of stupid things people do. People step in something nasty on the sidewalk; they slip on wet floors; they sit in wet paint—but never, since the creation of the heavens and earth, indeed of the very universe itself, has there ever been anything so stupid as the moment when Derek Ferretti tripped on his own shoelace and fell off of a speeding Russian train.

Derek didn't have the chance to yell as much as the word "Timber!" as he keeled over like a felled tree and slipped into the wind. His butt bounced on the edge of the car, giving him a nasty bruise, and his foot wedged itself tightly under the rope that tied the bulldozer to the train. He twisted his body, and in an instant the whole world turned backward and upside down as he hung there, dangling from the train head-first by one foot. Now came the time for screaming.

"Annnnaaaaa!" he yelled. Anna woke and came to him, but there wasn't much she could do. Derek could see the powerful wheels of the train spinning like buzz saws inches away from his face. His trapped foot was the only thing keeping the rest of his body from falling off into oblivion.

The wind lifted his dangling body up and down as he flailed his arms, trying to grab onto something. The pain from his twisting ankle grew as his body hung in space, whipping with the wind like a crazy American flag.

He caught a brief glimpse of Anna crying something desperately as she grabbed at the cuff of his pants. She was so upset, she was yelling half in Russian, half in English. Igor hopped out of the bulldozer scoop to help, but to no avail. At the absolute mercy of the wind and the train, Derek's hair grazed the edge of the train's wheels and he realized that this was no mere pop quiz of life—this may well have been his final exam.

Derek felt his hope slipping away as his trapped foot began to slip out of his untied high-top. There would be no trip to Romania for him. No meeting with Yuri Shafiroff. Who would have thought that his life would end because of the shoelaces of his Reeboks?

"Annaaaaaaaa!" he screamed as his foot flew free from his sneaker. For an instant he could see the horrified faces of Anna and Igor disappearing into the distance, as Derek fell from the train, to meet his destiny.

CHAPTER 16

Twenty-one Miles of The Dragon

It didn't happen the way it happens in James Bond movies. If James Bond ever got thrown from a train, he would brush himself off, find a very fast horse, and catch up with the train in a matter of seconds.

Derek felt every last stone as he rolled through the gravel and grass at the edge of the tracks. When he stopped rolling, he looked up just in time to see the end of the train passing by.

Derek let out that awful angry roar reserved for moments that went beyond words. He hurled a handful of gravel after the train like an angry child.

"You suck!" he screamed at no one in particular, and then his brain suddenly realized the tremendous shock his body had been through, and Derek passed out.

CONCUSSIONS ARE freaky things. Derek knew about that because he had had a concussion after the car accident.

His body had felt awful, and his brain had taken a flying leap into left field for a while.

The concussion Derek received after falling off the train ranked a perfect ten as far as concussions go, which was not too good. If the car accident sent his brain on a line drive into left field, this time it was smacked clear out of the ballpark.

When Derek came to, things weren't quite right with the world. For one thing, his head felt like someone was inside it, tap-dancing with cleats on. Second, it seemed gravity didn't pull him in the proper direction; it was a chore to keep his balance, and his dizziness simply wouldn't go away. Third, Derek's mind seemed to have switched into the energy-saver mode. He had a very severe—but, he hoped, temporary—brownout of the brain. He felt very slow—slow to think, slow to act, slow to remember.

Above him the sky didn't seem the right shade of blue; the ground beneath him didn't feel right; his eyes couldn't focus properly, and the air didn't even smell the way air should. The whole universe seemed to have shifted one degree out of whack.

He stood in his stocking feet, trying to keep his balance and to balance his thoughts. It was no easy task.

"*You're an embarrassment,*" he heard his mother say.

Was he? Yes, he was. Why? Why? Well, there certainly had to be a reason why. Yes, there was a reason. It was because he had fallen off a train. He was trying to take Anna to . . .

He was trying to take Anna where?

Was that today?

Was that just a dream?

No, it was today and it was real. He was trying to take Anna to . . . to . . .

Well, wherever he was trying to take her, he had

loused it up real good. He couldn't do anything right, could he?

Derek looked up into the sky. How long ago had he fallen off the train?

Weren't they traveling with a friend?

It looked like it was late morning already.

Who were they traveling with?

Yes, it was late morning, perhaps even early afternoon. By now Anna had reached Kiev and, if all went well, she was already on her way to . . . to . . . to wherever she was supposed to be going.

Derek had failed her. He had screwed up, as usual.

"Your father would be ashamed of you," his mother said from inside his brain. Derek wondered how on earth his mother had gotten in there.

"Shut up, Mom," he told her. She just shook her head and sighed.

Igor!

That was his name: Igor. He had been on the train with them. There. That proved it. Derek didn't have amnesia or anything, because he could remember everyone's name. Even if he couldn't remember where he was taking Anna, or even why he had left Spaso House in the first place.

Looking himself over, Derek found many cuts and bruises. His ankle hurt and must have been sprained slightly.

"Too weird," Derek heard his sister say. *"I've got the weirdest brother in the world."*

"Can it!" said Derek. No wonder his head hurt so much, what with so many people occupying his brain today.

He shook his head. People occupying his brain? That didn't quite make sense, but he let it go. It didn't matter.

Fighting the strangely spinning world and shifting

gravity, Derek found both his high-tops by the side of the railroad tracks. Apparently the other one had been thrown off his foot by the force of his fall. He put them on and began his journey to find . . . to find what?

A dragon.

Yes, that's right. It was a dragon he was hunting down. A dragon that couldn't bear to see Derek succeed. A dragon that couldn't bear the sight of Derek actually kissing the most wonderful girl in the whole world. A dragon that . . .

Breaks windows.

Broken windows! Something about broken windows. In Spaso House. He could hear them breaking in his mind. It seemed like another lifetime. Maybe it was.

Damn you! He screamed at The Dragon that seemed to be ruling his life. *It's your fault! Everything's your fault!*

Yes, The Dragon was near. It had pulled Derek off the train to do battle. A fight to the death—and not Anna, nor Igor, nor all the people tap-dancing in Derek's brain could be a part of this battle. Derek had to fight The Dragon alone, or never be free of it.

In his half-dream state, Derek found that all of this made a great deal of sense.

THE SOVIET countryside was immense. It seemed to go on forever in all directions. There was not a soul to be seen. He stumbled along the train tracks for an hour, but no trains came by. Soon he turned down a narrow dirt path through endless hills of prickly bushes and trees. Not a soul. What would he have done if he found somebody?

"The Dragon," said Ralphy Sherman, who also had made his way into Derek's brain for the day, *"likes to spoon out people's eyeballs and serve them in borscht."*

Derek ignored him.

The day wore on. Two hours and still no sign of life. Derek knew he would not see another human being until he had reached the battleground.

Now, where had he been headed on that train with Anna? He knew it would come to him sooner or later. He wondered what she and Igor had done after Derek fell off the train. Did they give themselves up in Kiev, and send someone to rescue him, or did they go through with the plan? No doubt, whatever decisions and adventures Igor and Anna were going through were not easy.

The path before him got narrower and vanished, so Derek took to blazing his own trail, beating the bush before him with a stick to chase away any Soviet rattlesnakes and things like that. He ignored the various people talking in his head, and tried to forget about the pain in his ankle.

THE FIRST farmhouse Derek came to was empty. It was old and the whitewash had been worn off by countless winters. Inside the floorboards were rotten and the ragged remnants of furniture littered the floor—mildewed upholstery, broken chairs.

Out back there was a well, but it was dry. Seeing the well made Derek realize just how thirsty he was. He couldn't remember the last time he had had anything to drink, not to mention anything to eat. He was famished as well.

"So," Derek said to The Dragon, "You're going to starve me to death? You're going to make me die of thirst. You're going to kill me just like you killed my father." The Dragon answered with a silent laugh. Everyone else in his brain had something to say about it, too. The one voice mysteriously absent from his brain, however, was his father's, and that made Derek very uneasy.

DEREK REACHED the second farmhouse an hour later. It, too, was old and abandoned. This one had indoor plumbing, and Derek went right up to the kitchen faucet, his mouth preparing itself for the cool fresh water. The faucet gurgled, wheezed, wheezed some more, then coughed up a bit of mud and died. No water there. No people there. No dragon. It was already late in the afternoon when Derek set off across the overgrown field toward another farmhouse in the distance.

IT WAS at the third farmhouse that Derek began to worry and question a whole lot of things. By now the voices in his head had quieted down some, and Derek had regained enough of his senses to realize that all those voices were simply a part of his concussion and nothing more. It was late in the day now—perhaps four or five in the afternoon. The sun was still high in the sky, but Derek knew he had been traveling a long time. This third farmhouse was bigger than the other two. Here, there were signs of life—a chicken coop, a barnyard. Derek stepped up to the door and knocked. No answer. He knocked again, then turned the knob. It was unlocked, so he went in.

Inside were musty furnishings—a couch, chairs, tables—all covered with dust.

In the kitchen were pots and pans. Vegetables lay in a corner, old and rotted. On the grill was a pan encrusted with something that might have once been ham. The table was set with three plates and silverware. One plate had an ancient egg on it. All three plates were covered with several years' supply of dust.

This was all very strange.

It made Derek wonder if perhaps there was something he was missing—something he wasn't thinking about—something his scrambled, bruised mind couldn't get a handle on during its present brownout.

Perhaps, thought Derek, perhaps things were worse than he imagined. After all, people just didn't leave things like this in a perfectly good farmhouse.

Derek thought back to the moment when he fell off the train. He had hit the ground hard. Very hard. He had passed out.

Maybe, just maybe, Derek had cashed in his chips when he fell off the train. Perhaps this is what happened to you when you died; you wandered the world forever. All alone.

It made a lot of sense in a weird, stomach-turning sort of way.

This farmhouse had no water either, and so, even more hungry and thirsty, Derek left the ghostly place.

He glanced at the chicken coop as he left. There were chickens, all right. They were dead. They had been dead for a very long time.

AT SIX o'clock that evening, the sun was still in the sky, and Derek had found a single-lane paved road that led out of the wilderness, toward some distant apartment buildings. Weeds grew through cracks in the middle of the road. There were a few homes along the road, but still no people. Derek didn't want to think about what that meant. Either he was dead, or everyone else was, and he was the only one left. Either way, it wasn't a pleasant thought and . . .

Yuri Shafiroff!

Yes! That was it! He had been taking Anna to see her father in . . . in Romania. His mind was slowly coming back to him . . . but the dizziness remained, along with that otherwordly feeling inside his head, and an overwhelming desire to fight The Dragon.

Derek limped slowly down the road, toward the distant buildings. This was not funny anymore—not that it had been funny to begin with, but now it was less funny than ever. He could almost smell The Dragon now. It was there waiting for him way down that road, near those distant apartment buildings.

THERE WAS broken glass everywhere. The twenty-story apartment buildings rose around him like skeletons. They were empty, and shards of glass, having fallen from the dark dead windows, lay strewn everywhere about Derek's feet, shining evilly in the dying sunlight. Derek could see the smokestacks of some infernal factory looming in the distance. This was an empty city. A dead city.

Derek stumbled between two of the buildings and found himself in a huge courtyard of concrete and broken glass. Weeds had pushed through the seams in the concrete, turning the courtyard into a checkerboard.

Where is everybody?

Why is it so quiet?

Why am I so alone?

Finally Derek dared to ask himself the questions he should have asked when he came across the three farmhouses. No answers came yet, except for the one answer he was waiting for.

Yes, this was the battleground. This was where The Dragon waited for him. Any minute now. Any minute.

But first, thought Derek, *I have to get a drink. I must have some water.*

He searched the side of a building, and found a spigot, which he turned on. Wonder of wonders, water began to pour out—first brown, then clear. He put his hands in it. It was cold and refreshing.

Any minute now . . .

Derek cupped his hands, and let them fill with the cool water. Slowly he brought the water to his lips.

And then it all clicked.

His mind snapped into place, and the truth came blasting to light so violently, so quickly, that Derek screamed in terror. He ripped his hands apart, letting the water splash to the ground before it had a chance to touch his lips.

No, it couldn't be. It couldn't!

Not a single soul. Anywhere.

Deserted. Abandoned.

Smokestacks! Oh, how could he have been so dim? How could he not have known? They weren't smoke-stacks; they were cooling towers. They didn't belong to a factory, they belonged to an awful place with a name known to everyone on the planet Earth.

Those distant towers belonged to a power plant.

And the name of the power plant was *Chernobyl.*

Derek screamed again, but no one heard him. No one for twenty-one miles in any direction, for when the radioactive core of the infamous nuclear power plant had melted down, the area had been completely evacuated. Forever.

Derek staggered to the middle of the huge lonely courtyard, still screaming as if he had been dipped in molten lava. He frantically tried to brush the radioactive water from his hands, but he couldn't. He wiped it on his pants and on the ground, but it wouldn't go away. It was on his hands; it was in the air. It was in his clothes; it was all over his skin—in his mouth, in his nose, in his lungs, in his blood.

There was no dragon here, only death. Death was

around him, squeezing into him, filling his body. There was no escape—nowhere to hide. It was touching his hands; it was blowing through his hair. Death was as close as his own bedroom, as close as his father's car.

It didn't go away, and he couldn't run from it no matter how many trains he took. Derek fell to his knees, and closed his eyes.

"Damn you for doing it!" Derek screamed. "Damn you for killing my father! Damn you damn you damn you!"

"Damn it, Derek, you never listen to a word I say!" yelled Derek's father, as they drove along the highway in Chicago. "I tell you something, and you go right ahead and do whatever you want anyway!"

"You don't understand," said Derek, refusing to look at his father. He just stared out of the windshield. "If I hadn't gone to the stadium at six A.M.*, we would never have gotten tickets to the concert! People kill for tickets to see the Slugs in concert!"*

Mr. Ferretti was red in the face with anger. "And you could have been killed! Do you have any idea how dangerous it was?" Just the thought of it made him step on the accelerator harder.

"I can take care of myself!" answered Derek.

"That's a bad neighborhood you were in!"

"I was with friends!"

"Those sleazy friends of yours aren't worth my spit!"

"They're not sleazy!" said Derek, raising his voice even louder. "You think anyone who has an earring is sleazy! Well, I've got news for you: I'm getting my ear pierced, too!"

Mr. Ferretti took his eyes off the road and snapped his head to Derek. "You will not!" He growled.

"I have a right!"

"Not while you're my son!"

"It's a free country!" screamed Derek.

"That's it!" yelled Mr. Ferretti, flooring his car through the red light he never saw. "I'm grounding you for—"

"Dad!" Derek shouted, his anger leaving him as he saw the red light a second too late.

The world exploded from the left. Neither of them saw the color of the car that hit them. Derek screamed.

He screamed long and loud, screaming to the lonely skeleton towers of the deserted Russian square. His scream sifted through all those thousands of jagged windows. Finally the truth rocketed home with amazing accuracy. It was an awful truth Derek thought he had left in Chicago—a truth he thought he could ward off by keeping busy, by blaming his mother, by taking Anna's problems on as his own. By blaming The Dragon.

Derek raised his cry to the empty Soviet skies. "It's my fault," he wailed. "It's my fault. It was all along!"

He had broken the windows at Spaso House. *He* had fallen off the train because of his own clumsiness. *He* had caused his father's death. Not any dragon. He had killed his father.

If he hadn't been contrary.

If he hadn't been shallow and stupid.

If.

He had been running from the blame for too long, but here he was, at the very edge of the world, and there was nowhere else to run.

How could he live with it? Better to crumble into a ball and disappear from the face of the earth than to bear the blame.

If things had been different.

If he could do it over again.

If.

"Dad," he said as the tears that wouldn't flow at his

father's funeral finally came. "Dad, take away this awful feeling. Show me what to do. Get me out of this horrible place." But still, as before, there came no answer from his father. "Please. . . ."

And then, something occurred to Derek.

Perhaps he was asking the wrong question.

Derek thought hard and dug down, searching for the question. What did he really want from his father? What did he need more than anything else in the world? More than guidance, more than answers, more than consolation?

He picked through the darkest parts of his mind, and came up with a single simple plea.

"Dad," he cried. "I'm sorry, Dad. Forgive me." He said it out loud, and his words echoed between the skeleton buildings.

All was silent.

Derek felt the breeze and the poisoned air blowing across his skin, rippling in his ears, sifting through all the broken windows, and when the breeze was gone, something was different. Something had changed.

Derek's thoughts—his feelings—seemed somehow to have order again, as if everything inside him had fallen back into place.

But that wasn't all.

In a moment Derek heard a whisper. A distant soft whisper, that sounded almost like his father's voice. *Huff-huff-huff*, it said, calmly and regularly. *Thud-thud-thud*, it said as it got louder. Derek opened his eyes, and looked around.

The helicopter rose away from the two reactors of Chernobyl that still were operating, just a speck in the distant sky. It wasn't coming in Derek's direction, but it was close enough. Derek wiped his eyes and snapped back into the here-and-now. He rose to his feet and began to wave his hands, slowly at first, then frantically, screaming, "I'm here, I'm here, down here!" Although the sun was getting low in the sky, Derek knew that a boy in a red shirt jumping up and down in the middle of a huge concrete courtyard would be hard to miss.

Sure enough, the helicopter changed course toward the apartment buildings. Derek jumped and waved his arms and yelled.

The helicopter circled twice, curiously, as if not sure what to do, and finally it descended and set down across the courtyard. Derek ran toward it.

"Eto zapreschonnaya territoriya!" shouted the pilot. Derek quickly climbed aboard. The two men on board spewed questions at him in Russian.

"I'm an American," said Derek.

The pilot looked at his copilot warily, and then shut the door, motioning for Derek to sit down.

As they rose above the dead courtyard, Derek closed his eyes and relaxed, feeling his headache start to slip away—perhaps for good.

Derek never knew whether or not that helicopter was an answer from his father, but that didn't matter. The feeling he had inside was answer enough.

CHAPTER 17

The Man Behind the Curtain

As Derek was led down the long hall, toward the huge double doors, he had a strange sense of fear. The place overwhelmed him. It was those high ceilings that did it, and those larger-than-life pictures on the wall.

On the hall's left wall was a full-length portrait of Lenin, among crowds of workers—but, as Derek looked closer, he could see it wasn't a portrait, but a handmade carpet. It must have taken months to create.

On the right wall were portraits of all the leaders of the Soviet Union since Lenin. Khrushchev, Brezhnev . . . they were all there. All but Stalin—his picture was completely absent from the wall.

Beside Derek, the guard who escorted him showed no emotion whatsoever.

Derek swallowed hard. *Don't be scared*, he told himself. *There's nothing to worry about.* Still, his knees felt weak. He wondered if that was a symptom of radiation exposure, but even as he thought it, he knew it wasn't the case.

Waiting for word from the doctor as he had sat there in the hospital had been terrifying. It had been only two days ago, but it already seemed like a month.

His mother had flown down to be with him.

Derek thought that would be the worst thing of all, having to face his mother, but it wasn't what he expected.

He was sitting in a chair by the hospital-room window when his mom arrived, only an hour or so after they had admitted him. She didn't have Philip to do her talking and feeling for her. She faced Derek alone.

Derek figured she'd say something like "You've got a lot of explaining to do, young man," but she didn't. Instead she came right up to him and hugged him; not one of her half-human hugs, either. She didn't let him go for a long time. It was then that Derek realized while he had been gone, his mother had been fighting her own dragons.

She looked Derek in the eye, and the first thing she said was, "Anna's in Romania, with her father."

Derek breathed a long-overdue sigh of relief, but also of regret. The fact that Anna had made it was wonderful. The fact that Derek might never see her again was miserable. Still, he knew that, in the long run, his own misery was unimportant. The thought comforted him. Sort of.

"You should have told me what you were doing," said his mom. "It was very . . ."

Very what? thought Derek. *Very stupid? Very immature? Very irresponsible?*

". . . it was very brave," she said, and then, again looking him right in the eye, she said, "I'm sorry, Derek." She began to pace the room, trying to figure out what she wanted to say. It took a long time for her to get it out.

"You know," she said, "it's not easy being an ambassador and your mother at the same time. I guess it's never been easy being you, either. I'm sorry, Derek. I'm sorry for a lot of things."

"So am I, Mom," answered Derek.

She hugged him again, not wanting to let go, and Derek realized how wonderful it was to have a mother. Perhaps his mom was just now realizing how wonderful it was to have a son.

Together the two of them waited for the doctor to tell them how Derek would be affected by the radiation.

Now, two days later, Derek walked down the endless hall.

I should consider myself lucky, thought Derek. *It's not everyday that someone gets a private meeting with Mikhail Gorbachev, the General Secretary of the Communist Party*. It was true. To be granted a meeting with him, you had to have done something big. Something wonderful—or terrible.

The double doors of the inner office loomed closer, as Derek and the guard approached. The guard opened the door to reveal an office with red carpeting and off-white walls. There was a large desk in the office, and everything on the desk was in perfect order, as if glued there.

Behind the desk sat a round-faced balding man in a dark blue suit, a man Derek recognized from the news. He hung up one of the five rotary phones on his desk as Derek entered.

"Mr. Ferretti," he said, almost smiling. "So we finally meet! Please, sit." His accent was very strong.

He shook Derek's hand, and Derek sat down across

from the most important man in the Soviet Union. To Derek and any other American, he *was* the Soviet Union.

"So," said Secretary Gorbachev, "are you well?"

"Yeah," said Derek. "The doctor said I wasn't there long enough to get much radiation. I didn't eat or drink anything there, so I'm OK."

"Good," Mr. Gorbachev said, leaning back in his chair. He was silent for a moment, then said, "I am thinking that you do not know what trouble you have caused. Do you?"

How was Derek supposed to answer that? "I think so," he said.

"Well, think once more," said Gorbachev, as he dropped a pile of newspapers in front of Derek. "Please read," he said. Derek had already seen the headlines in the American papers. He didn't want to see them again.

AMBASSADOR'S SON FREES DISSIDENT'S DAUGHTER

read one headline. Another one read:

SHAFIROFF GIRL RAILROADED BY JUNIOR DIPLOMAT

and yet another headline read:

PUPPY LOVE SHATTERS IRON CURTAIN

"*Glasnost* is one thing," said Gorbachev, "but this?"

Derek grimaced. How embarrassing! Derek saw his own tenth-grade picture and a picture of Anna with her father. Anna was wearing his Bulls jacket.

"One newspaper claims that you planned the whole thing with the CIA," said Gorbachev. "Even *we* know that is not true!"

Derek smiled in embarrassment. The General Secretary leaned back in his chair.

"You think it is funny?" asked Secretary Gorbachev. "Maybe you think this is funny, too." He tossed an official-looking document into Derek's lap. It was in Russian.

"What is this?" asked Derek.

"It is Anna Shafiroff's exit visa!" was the answer. "Do you think we have no heart? I had personally signed it! It was our plan to send Anna quietly to her father and make everything easy for everyone. "I didn't know."

"And now you are this big hero, yes? Causing trouble for everybody!" complained the General Secretary. "You cause trouble even in my own family. My fourteen-year-old niece, even she is a fan of yours now!"

"Really?" said Derek, smiling. "What's her name?"

Secretary Gorbachev pretended he didn't hear that. "This puts you and me in a very difficult position," he said. "Our official policy is to expel you from the country."

Derek bit his lip and kept his mouth shut. *Don't sweat*, he thought. *Keep calm.*

"But," said the General Secretary, "your mother is a very popular ambassador. She personally appealed to me to keep you in the Soviet Union."

Derek nodded.

"So, out of respect for your mother—to spare her the shame of what you have done—we offer you an alternative. We will look the other way, for your mother's sake, and allow you to stay, under one condition. . . ."

Derek, all ears, sat and listened to the General Secretary's proposal.

* * *

In the outer office, on the other end of the long hall, sat Derek's mom, Dayna, and Philip. For once, his mom was sitting quietly, rather than rushing around.

When they saw Derek, they all stood, as if greeting a diplomat.

"Did he pardon you, Derek?" asked his mom. "What did he say?"

Derek was quiet for a moment. He thought about Anna with her father, far away. He had done something good by getting her on that train; he was certain of that. For once he had done something for someone else—he had risked his life for her, and he wasn't ashamed of it. He had done something he believed in, hadn't he? That was something to be proud of, wasn't it?

"He wants me to apologize," said Derek. "He wants me to sign a piece of paper that says I'm sorry and I'm ashamed, and all that; then he wants me to read it on Russian TV. If I do, they'll accept the apology, and let me stay in the country."

His mother smiled, a heavy burden lifted from her head. "I was worried for a while," she said, relieved beyond words. "I'm so happy for you, Derek!" She turned around. "Philip!"

He hopped to his feet.

"Call the embassy—tell them I'll be in before lunch, and tell them—"

"Mom," Derek interrupted. He began to feel sick to his stomach, as if his brain, his heart, and his guts were in complete disagreement with each other. Now he knew how Yuri Shafiroff must have felt. "Mom, I'm not going to do it."

That hit everyone like a slap in the face. His mother turned to him. "What?"

"I'm not sorry, Mom. If I apologized and said I was

sorry, I'd be lying. I'm not sorry—I'm glad I helped Anna."

His mother was speechless. Her jaw was open a good ten seconds before any words came out. "Derek, this is no time to be contrary," she finally said. "Sign the stupid thing and let's go. Please, Derek, it's only . . ."

"It's only what, Mom? It's only words? Words don't mean anything? Words aren't important?" Derek stared at her, and she looked away. He had stared his mother down. Once before, Derek had apologized against his will, but that seemed like a different lifetime, and Derek could not do that again. And it had nothing to do with being contrary.

She paced across to the other side of the room in silence. If the air had been any heavier, the walls would have buckled out.

Finally she turned to him once more. "You do what you feel is right, Derek," she said, slowly. "I can't make the decision for you."

Derek looked at Philip. He always used to have an answer, but not this time. It was Derek's decision, and his decision was already made. Derek turned to his sister, and she spoke, very quietly.

"I wish I had your guts." It was the nicest thing his sister had ever said to him.

Before Derek turned to go back to the General Secretary, his mother grabbed him and gave him a strong hug. He thought she might try to discourage him one more time, but she didn't. Instead she gazed at him, and, with a slim smile, she gently said, "You're so much like your father." She kissed him on the forehead, took a step away from him, and Derek saw a moistness about her eyes that he knew would have been tears if she wasn't an ambassador. "Go ahead," she said. "We'll be waiting for you when you come out."

* * *

THE LONG hall seemed much shorter as Derek marched to the General Secretary's office a second time.

The guard let him in, and again Mr. Gorbachev put down one of his five phone receivers. Derek handed him the paper.

"But you have forgotten to sign . . . ," said Mr. Gorbachev as he glanced at the apology.

"No, I didn't forget," said Derek. "I'm sorry for messing up your plans—I'm really sorry about that—but I'm not ashamed of what I did. I'll never be ashamed of it."

Mr. Gorbachev was as shocked as his mother had been. "You would rather be expelled from the country than apologize?"

Derek began to feel sick to his stomach again, but that would pass. As much as he wanted to stay, he knew he would much rather live with his aunt and uncle in Chicago than live in Spaso House without his principles.

"I guess so," Derek answered.

General Secretary Gorbachev stared at him sternly, but when Derek didn't crack, the sternness was replaced with a "why me?" sort of expression—the look of a busy man who was overworked and didn't need this aggravation.

Mr. Gorbachev sighed, and gazed at Derek—not in anger, but with an honest understanding.

"Nothing's ever easy, is it?" he said.

Derek had to agree.

CHAPTER 18

No Place Like Home

Dearest Derek,

There is no way to thank you for all you have done. My father and I are both grateful to you. I am glad to hear that you are well, but sorry to hear about all the trouble you've gone through on my behalf.

Did you know that my father cried when he first saw me? It is wonderful to be with him again, and I couldn't be happier. My father is a very sad and troubled man—not at all like I remember. I don't know if I'll ever know all that he thinks about, but that's all right. We are together, that pleases him greatly. Things can only get better. My only regret is that Romania is so far away from you in Moscow . . .

"So, YOU'VE been expelled from the country!" said Igor. "Hah! You have it easy. Thirty years ago, you would have mysteriously vanished, never to be seen again!"

Actually, it was Igor who had it easy. It turned out that Igor, left on the train with Anna, had risen to the occasion, switching trains in Kiev, and somehow evading the border guards. He made it all the way to Romania with Anna, and he had even met Yuri Shafiroff. "We talked," Igor had told Derek. "He has interesting ideas. I will give them some thought when I become General Secretary."

Igor had managed to dodge in and out of shadows, somehow making his way back to Moscow three days later, getting nothing more than a severe scolding and an eternal grounding from his parents, who decided it was best for everyone to keep the whole thing their little secret. No one else ever knew that Igor was a part of Anna's trip.

"So, if you're expelled, when do they expel you?" Igor asked, as he practiced spinning a basketball on his finger.

"When they get around to it," said Derek. It had been over a month since they had "officially expelled" him, but no one had come around to physically throw him out yet. "They're busy in the Kremlin," said Derek. "They don't have the time to waste on a dissident American like me."

Actually, Derek couldn't really be considered a dissident anymore. Since he had gotten back, he had been as cooperative as could be. He was starting to like being agreeable—perhaps it was because people were beginning to respect his thoughts and opinions a bit more. He even began to enjoy those stuffy parties and dinners his mother gave; people actually laughed at his jokes! Incredible though it might sound, he was becoming a regular gentleman. He had to be one—after all, he was the ambassador's son. It was getting hard to imagine what life would have been like right now, if his father had still been alive. No doubt Derek would still be ranting on about rock concerts and earrings and a whole host of silly topics. Still, he thought of his father often, and when the need arose, Derek had a good talk with him.

Igor gave up trying to spin the ball, and began dribbling it down the street. The afternoon streets were always packed with people, some of whom gave Igor a dirty look as he dribbled around them, but people were getting used to it. They were getting used to basketballs, skateboards, roller skates, and the like. Derek had begun to see more of them in the streets now that it was summer. But it was more than just the summer—so many things were changing in Eastern Europe: There was talk of the Berlin Wall coming down, and people were openly discussing the possibility of Ukrainian independence. Even Igor had gotten rid of his red Young Pioneer scarf! Derek sensed hope and excitement all around him . . . but also a bit of fear. Much would have to be broken before anything could be fixed.

"Hey, where are you going?" said Igor, as Derek turned down a side street.

"Just taking a short cut," answered Derek.

"That's no short cut!" said Igor, knowing where Derek's little detour would take them. "We have no time—Fyodor and the others will be waiting for us."

But Derek didn't stop, so Igor had to follow. Fyodor could live without Derek for five minutes; at that moment, he was probably beating some other poor slob in a game of one-on-one. Fyodor had never asked Derek for that favor Derek owed him—at least not yet. Derek had come to learn that Fyodor collected favors the way American kids collected baseball cards.

"Favors will soon be the most important commodity

in the Soviet Union," Fyodor had told him. "As long as I am owed a favor, I will never be without a friend."

Derek finally arrived at his destination.

"I knew you were coming here," said Igor, shaking his head. To a stranger, the building before them would have looked like any other apartment building in Moscow, but to Derek it was a memory that held too many confused emotions: joy and disaster, love and anger. Memories of imaginary dragons, and of a very real girl. It was Anna's old apartment building.

Igor dribbled the basketball impatiently as Derek looked up at the gray building.

"You know, we still write to each other," said Derek. It was true, but the letters were getting shorter each time. He guessed neither of them was much when it came to writing.

"Maybe you'll see her again," offered Igor.

"Maybe." Maybe he would visit her in Romania someday. Maybe he would meet her father. Maybe he would kiss her again.

"Anyway," said Igor, "you know what they say: 'There's plenty of squid in the sea.' And I hear General Secretary Gorbachev's niece likes you; she might even be watching the basketball game today!"

Derek could have stared at the building all day, but Igor wouldn't let him. He hurried off. "C'mon, let's go!"

Before Derek followed, he took a moment to look around, and to take a deep breath of the Moscow air. It was a bit smoky from all the cars, and a bit damp from the morning's rain. He would miss that smell when they sent him away.

If they sent him away.

Oddly enough, most people seemed to have forgotten

all about Derek's flight with Anna, now that it was out of the news.

No, they couldn't send him away now, there were so many things he still had to do in Moscow—like winning the friendships of all those kids at the Anglo-American school, kids he never even gave a chance to be his friend. And beating Igor in chess. And beating Fyodor in one-on-one. Well, perhaps if Derek kept being good, they might not get around to throwing him out for a long time . . . like maybe until after his next year at school . . .

. . . And maybe, if he was very, very lucky, they'd never get around to it.

Derek smiled. With his shoelaces tied, and luck on his side, things would work out fine.

Derek turned and dashed down the cobblestone street after Igor, leaving Anna's apartment building, and a great many other things, behind.

"Hey, Igor," he called, as he hurried to catch up with his friend. "About Gorbachev's niece . . . what was her name again?"

MORE TOR CLASSICS

☐	50440-2	DAISY MILLER *Henry James*	$2.50 Canada $3.25
☐	50448-8	DOCTOR JEKYLL AND MR. HYDE *Robert Louis Stevenson*	$2.50 Canada $3.25
☐	50442-9	DRACULA *Bram Stoker*	$2.50 Canada $3.25
☐	50455-0	EDGAR ALLEN POE: A Collection of Short Stories *Edgar Allen Poe*	$2.50 Canada $3.25
☐	50457-7	FRANKENSTEIN *Mary Shelley*	$2.50 Canada $3.25
☐	50459-3	THE HOUSE OF THE SEVEN GABLES *Nathaniel Hawthorne*	$2.50 Canada $3.25
☐	50467-4	THE INVISIBLE MAN *H. G. Wells*	$2.50 Canada $3.25
☐	50471-2	JOURNEY TO THE CENTER OF THE EARTH *Jules Verne*	$2.50 Canada $3.25
☐	50469-0	THE JUNGLE BOOKS *Rudyard Kipling*	$2.50 Canada $3.25
☐	50473-9	KIDNAPPED *Robert Louis Stevenson*	$2.50 Canada $3.25
☐	51956-6	THE LADY OR THE TIGER and Other Short Stories *Frank Stockton*	$2.50 Canada $3.25

Buy them at your local bookstore or use this handy coupon:
Clip and mail this page with your order.

Publishers Book and Audio Mailing Service
P.O. Box 120159, Staten Island, NY 10312-0004

Please send me the book(s) I have checked above. I am enclosing $ ______________
(Please add $1.25 for the first book, and $.25 for each additional book to cover postage and handling. Send check or money order only—no CODs.)

Name ______________________________
Address ______________________________
City ______________________ State/Zip ______________________
Please allow six weeks for delivery. Prices subject to change without notice.

READ TOR CLASSICS

☐	52297-4	THE LAST OF THE MOHICANS *James Fenimore Cooper*	$3.99 Canada $4.99
☐	50475-5	THE LEGEND OF SLEEPY HOLLOW *Washington Irving*	$2.50 Canada $3.25
☐	52333-4	LITTLE WOMEN *Louisa May Alcott*	$3.99 Canada $4.50
☐	52076-9	O PIONEERS! *Willa Cather*	$2.50 Canada $3.25
☐	52336-9	PRIDE AND PREJUDICE *Jane Austen*	$2.50 Canada $3.25
☐	50477-1	THE PRINCE AND THE PAUPER *Mark Twain*	$2.50 Canada $3.25
☐	50479-8	THE RED BADGE OF COURAGE *Stephen Crane*	$2.50 Canada $3.25
☐	52332-6	RIP VAN WINKLE and Other Stories *Washington Irving*	$2.50 Canada $3.25
☐	50482-8	ROBINSON CRUSOE *Daniel Defoe*	$2.50 Canada $3.25
☐	50483-6	THE SCARLET LETTER *Nathaniel Hawthorne*	$2.50 Canada $3.25
☐	50501-8	THE SECRET GARDEN *Frances Hodgson Burnett*	$3.99 Canada $4.99

Buy them at your local bookstore or use this handy coupon:
Clip and mail this page with your order.

Publishers Book and Audio Mailing Service
P.O. Box 120159, Staten Island, NY 10312-0004

Please send me the book(s) I have checked above. I am enclosing $ ______________
(Please add $1.25 for the first book, and $.25 for each additional book to cover postage and handling. Send check or money order only—no CODs.)

Name ________________________________
Address ______________________________
City ____________________ State/Zip ____________________

Please allow six weeks for delivery. Prices subject to change without notice.